In a moment Eliza was at the river's edge.

Haley was right behind. Eliza leaped onto an ice floe. The danger and daring of this action made Sam, Andy, and even Haley cry out. The huge chunk of ice on which Eliza landed creaked under her. With desperate energy, she leaped to another, then another. She slipped and stumbled, springing up again. Her shoes were gone. Her stockings were cut from her feet. Blood marked every step.

A Background Note about *Uncle Tom's Cabin*

Uncle Tom's Cabin opens in 1850, soon after the US Congress passed the Fugitive Slave Act, which made it a crime to assist a runaway slave. The Underground Railroad, a secret network of people who helped slaves escape from the slave-holding South to the North, remained active. Runaways received food and shelter at the Railroad's "stations," escape-route stops that totaled in the thousands. Slaves who were sold "down river" moved in the direction opposite of freedom. They were taken down the Mississippi River and sold to someone, usually a plantation owner, in the deep South. In 1865 the Thirteenth Amendment to the Constitution abolished slavery throughout the United States.

HARRIET BEECHER STOWE

UNCLE TOM'S CABIN

Edited, and with an Afterword,
by Joan Dunayer

TP THE TOWNSEND LIBRARY

UNCLE TOM'S CABIN

TP THE TOWNSEND LIBRARY

For more titles in the Townsend Library,
visit our website: **www.townsendpress.com**

All new material in this edition is
copyright © 2005 by Townsend Press.
Printed in the United States of America

0 9 8 7 6 5 4 3 2

Illustrations © 2006 by Hal Taylor

Townsend Press, Inc.
439 Kelley Drive
West Berlin, New Jersey 08091

ISBN-13: 978-1-59194-055-5
ISBN-10: 1-59194-055-9

Library of Congress Control Number:
2005929902

CONTENTS

CHAPTER 1

On a chilly November afternoon in 1850, Kentucky slave owner Arthur Shelby and Mississippi slave trader Daniel Haley were sitting in Shelby's well-furnished dining room. With their chairs almost touching, they earnestly discussed business.

Haley was short and heavyset. He had coarse features and the swaggering air of a low-class man who is trying to elbow his way upward in the world. He wore a gaudy vest of many colors and a blue neckerchief with yellow dots. Rings bedecked his large, coarse hands. His heavy gold watch-chain had a bundle of large seals of many colors attached to it. During the conversation Haley flourished and jingled this bundle with evident satisfaction.

Shelby had a gentleman's appearance. His well-maintained house and high-quality furnishings indicated wealth. "That's the way I'd arrange the matter," Shelby said.

'I can't do business that way, Mr. Shelby. I can't," Haley said.

"Tom is an uncommon fellow. He's certainly worth that amount. He's sensible, capable, and honest. He manages my whole farm like clockwork."

"You mean he's honest as niggers* go," Haley said, helping himself to a glass of brandy.

"No. Tom is a good, steady, pious fellow. I trust him with everything I have—money, house, horses—and let him come and go around the country. He's honest and trustworthy in everything."

"Some people don't believe there's such a thing as a trustworthy nigger," Haley said, "but *I* do. In the last bunch I took to New Orleans there was a fellow who was gentle and quiet and who prayed a lot. He fetched me a good sum. I bought him cheaply from a man who had to sell out, so I made six hundred dollars on him. I consider religion a valuable thing in a nigger when it's genuine."

"Well, Tom's genuinely religious," Shelby said. "Last fall I let him go to Cincinnati alone to do business for me. I said, 'Tom, I trust you because you're a Christian. I know you wouldn't cheat me.' Sure enough, he came back and brought five hundred dollars. Some low fellows

---

*In the 1850s uneducated people (both white and black) often used the term *nigger* instead of *Negro*.

asked him, 'Why didn't you head to Canada?' Tom answered, 'Master trusted me.' A slave who heard the conversation told me that Tom said that. I'm sorry to part with Tom. You should consider him as covering everything that I owe you, and you *would* if you had any conscience."

"I've got about as much conscience as any businessman can afford—just enough to swear by," Haley joked. "I like to oblige friends, but I'm a little hard up this year." He sighed and poured some more brandy.

"Well then, what do you want, Haley?" Shelby asked after an uneasy silence.

"Do you have a boy or gal you can throw in with Tom?"

"None that I could easily spare. I wouldn't sell at all if I didn't have to. I don't like parting with any of my slaves."

The door opened, and a small quadroon* boy around four years old entered the room. He was beautiful and engaging. His black hair hung in silky curls around his round, dimpled face. His large dark eyes, full of intelligence, looked out from under thick, long lashes. He wore a robe of scarlet and yellow plaid, carefully made and neatly fitted. His manner combined confidence and shyness.

"Hello!" Shelby said. He whistled and tossed

Quadroon refers to someone with no "pure" black parent but at least one parent with some recent black ancestry.

a bunch of raisins toward the boy. "Pick them up!" The child scampered after the prize while Shelby laughed. "Come here," Shelby said. The child came up, and Shelby patted his curly head and chucked him under the chin. "Now show this gentleman how you can dance and sing." The boy sang in a rich, clear voice and, in time with the music, made comical movements with his hands, feet, and body.

"Bravo!" Haley said, throwing him a quarter of an orange.

"Now walk like old Uncle Vincent when he has rheumatism," Shelby said.

The child's flexible limbs instantly assumed the appearance of deformity. With his back humped and Shelby's cane in his hand, he hobbled around the room. His face was drawn into a sorrowful pucker. He pretended to spit right and left, in imitation of an old man.

Shelby and Haley laughed uproariously. "Now," Shelby said, "show us how Elder Robbins leads the reciting of psalms."

The boy drew his chubby face down to a formidable length and began nasally intoning a psalm with great gravity.

"Hurray! What a young one!" Haley said. "That kid's a case." Clapping his hand on Shelby's shoulder, he said, "I'll tell you what: throw in that kid, and I'll consider your debt paid."

The door was gently opened, and a quadroon woman around twenty-five years old entered the room. The boy resembled her so much that she clearly was his mother. She had the same large dark eyes with long lashes and the same ripples of silky black hair. She blushed as she saw Haley eye her in undisguised admiration. Her dress, of the neatest possible fit, showed her fine figure. Haley immediately noticed her delicate hands and slender ankles. She stopped and looked hesitantly at Shelby.

"Well, Eliza?" Shelby said.

"I was looking for Harry, sir." The boy bounded toward her, showing the spoils he had gathered in the skirt of his robe.

"Take him away, then," Shelby said. Eliza hastily withdrew, carrying Harry on her arm.

"By God," Haley said, "there's an article! You could make your fortune in New Orleans on that gal any day. I've seen people pay more than a thousand for gals not a bit handsomer."

"I don't want to make my fortune on her," Shelby said dryly. Desiring to redirect the conversation, he uncorked a bottle of wine and asked Haley's opinion of it.

"First-rate," Haley said. Slapping his hand on Shelby's shoulder, he said, "How much do you want for the gal? What'll you take for her?"

"She's not for sale," Shelby said. "My wife wouldn't part with her for her weight in gold."

"Oh, women always say such things because they have no head for numbers. Just show them how much jewelry someone's weight in gold will buy, and they'll see things differently."

"I said no, and I mean no," Shelby said.

"Well, you'll let me have the boy, won't you? I'll pay handsomely for him."

"What on earth do you want with the child?" Shelby asked.

"I have a friend who wants handsome boys to raise for the market. He'll sell them to be servants to the wealthy. It makes a place look good to have handsome boys open doors and wait on visitors. They fetch a good sum. This little devil is so comical and musical, he's just the article!"

"I'd rather not sell him," Shelby said thoughtfully. "I'm a humane man. I'd hate to take the boy from his mother."

"You would, would you? Well, I can understand how you wouldn't want to hear a woman screeching the way they can. What if you send the gal away for a day and I take the boy then, when she isn't around? To make up with your wife, you could get her some earrings, or a new gown, or some such thing."

"No," Shelby said.

"Come now. These niggers aren't like white folks. They get over things. I'm not hard like some slave dealers. I've seen some fellows who can pull a woman's child right out of her arms and sell the child while she's screeching. That's bad policy. It damages the mother. Sometimes it makes her unfit for service. I knew a handsome gal in New Orleans who was ruined by that sort of handling. The fellow who bought her didn't want her baby. She squeezed her child in her arms and carried on in an awful way. When they carried off the child, the mother went mad. A clear waste of a thousand dollars. Poor management. It's always best to do the humane thing." Haley leaned back in his chair and folded his arms with an air of virtue. "Ted Loker, my old partner, would crack gals over the head and knock them around when they started hollering. I told him that just ruins the gals. It makes them sickly and sometimes ugly. It also makes it harder to break them in. Humaneness pays better. Still, I don't see anything wrong with selling a young one while the mother's away. White women are brought up to expect to keep their children, but niggers that are raised right know not to expect such things."

"Then, mine haven't been raised right," Shelby said.

"I guess not. You Kentucky folks spoil your niggers. You mean well by them, but you aren't doing them any favors. Niggers get sold to God knows who, so you're not doing them any favors if you give them notions and expectations instead of preparing them for what's to come. I bet your niggers would fall apart in some places where a Louisiana or Mississippi nigger would be singing and dancing for joy. So, what do you say?"

"I'll think it over and discuss the matter with my wife."

"Alright, but I'm in a hurry. I want to know as soon as possible." Haley rose and put on his overcoat.

"Come back this evening between six and seven, and you'll have my answer," Shelby said. Haley bowed and left. Shelby thought, "I would have liked to kick him down the steps, but I owe the rascal money, so what's to be done?"

The needs of the helpless carry little weight against financial interests, especially when the helpless are regarded as things: property.

CHAPTER 2

In approaching the door, Eliza had overheard enough of the conversation to know that a slave trader was making offers to buy someone. She would have stopped at the door to listen after coming out, but her mistress had summoned her. Still, Eliza thought she had heard the trader make an offer for Harry. Her heart had pounded. She had pressed Harry so tightly against her that he had looked up into her face with concern.

"Eliza, girl, what ails you today?" Margaret Shelby asked when Eliza had upset the water pitcher, overturned a small table, and offered her mistress a nightgown instead of the silk dress she had told Eliza to bring from the wardrobe.

"Oh, Mistress!" Eliza cried, bursting into tears. She sat down in a chair and sobbed.

"Why, Eliza, what ails you, child?"

"A trader has been talking with Master in the parlor. I heard him," Eliza said.

"Well, silly child, so what?"

"Do you suppose Master would sell my Harry?"

Knowing nothing of her husband's debts, Margaret responded, "Sell him? No, you foolish girl! He wouldn't sell any of our slaves. Why would anyone want to buy Harry? Cheer up, and hook my dress. Braid and curl my hair the way you did the other day. And don't listen at doors anymore."

"You never would agree to Harry's being sold?" Eliza asked.

"Of course not. I'd as soon sell my own child. Really, Eliza, you're getting too proud of Harry. A trader can't visit without your thinking he wants to buy him."

Reassured, Eliza nimbly completed her mistress's dressing and grooming.

Margaret was a high-class, religious woman. Although her husband wasn't religious, he respected his wife's piety. What he dreaded most, after his conversation with Haley, was telling his wife.

CHAPTER 3

From girlhood Eliza had been brought up by her mistress as a favorite. Under Margaret's protection, Eliza had reached maturity without being sexually abused. She was married to George, a bright, talented mulatto* who was a slave on a neighboring estate. George and Eliza had been married in the Shelbys' parlor. Margaret had adorned Eliza's beautiful hair with orange blossoms, put a bridal veil on her head, and given her white gloves to wear. The wedding had included cake, wine, and admiring guests. Margaret highly approved of the marriage. Eliza and George were perfectly suited to each other.

For four years after their marriage the couple had seen each other frequently. George's master, Walter Harris, had hired him out to work in a factory where cloth was manufactured from hemp. The factory's owner, Robert Wilson, was a

---

Mulatto refers to someone with one white parent and one "pure" black parent.

good-natured elderly man. He had allowed George to come and go as he wished. George's skill, intelligence, and pleasant manner had made him the factory's foremost worker. Despite his lack of education, he had invented a machine for cleaning hemp.

Hearing about George's invention, Harris had ridden to the factory. Wilson had greeted Harris warmly and congratulated him on owning such a valuable slave. Harris had been waited on and shown George's invention. In high spirits, George had spoken so well, held himself so erect, and looked so handsome and manly that Harris had begun to feel an uneasy consciousness of George's superiority. How dare this slave hold his head up among gentlemen? He needed to be taken down a peg. To the astonishment of Wilson and his workers, Harris had suddenly demanded George's wages and announced his intention of taking George home.

"But, Mr. Harris," Wilson had said, "isn't this sudden?"

"What if it is? Doesn't the man belong to me?"

"We would be willing, sir, to increase his wages," Wilson had offered.

"No. I don't need to hire out any of my slaves," Harris had responded.

"But, sir, he seems especially suited to this business," Wilson had persisted.

"That may be," Harris had said. "He never seemed particularly suited to any work that *I* wanted him to do."

"He invented this machine," a worker had commented.

"Yes, a labor-saving machine," Harris had replied. "He *would* invent that, wouldn't he? A nigger will do anything to avoid work."

George had stood with his lips pressed together. His large dark eyes had flashed like hot coals. He might have given way to an angry outburst if Wilson hadn't touched his arm and whispered, "You have to do as he says, George. Go with him. We'll try to help you."

Harris had taken George home and forced him to do farm drudgery. A week later Wilson had visited Harris and tried to persuade him to let George return to the factory. But Harris wouldn't be swayed.

CHAPTER 4

Eliza was sitting on the veranda sewing when George entered. "George, I'm so glad you're here," she said. "Mistress will be gone for the afternoon. Come into my room. We'll have the time to ourselves." Eliza drew George into a small, neat bedroom that opened onto the veranda. The room had a closet and dresser; a pleasant window at which Eliza often sat singing and sewing; and a small bookcase with books, as well as knickknacks that had been Christmas gifts.

"Look how big Harry is," Eliza said proudly. Holding onto Eliza's skirt, Harry shyly regarded his father. "Isn't he beautiful?" Eliza said, kissing him.

"I wish he'd never been born," George said bitterly. "I wish *I'd* never been born." Surprised and upset, Eliza sat down. "I'm sorry I've upset you," George said tenderly. "I wish you never had seen me. You might have been happy."

"How can you talk like that? We were so

happy until Harris brought you back to his farm."

"Yes, we were." Drawing Harry onto his knee, George gazed intently into Harry's eyes and passed his hands through Harry's curls. "He's just like you, Eliza, and you're the most beautiful woman I've ever seen, and the best one I ever expect to see. But my life is nothing but drudgery now."

"I know how you feel about losing your place at the factory, and you have a hard master. Be patient, though. Maybe something..."

"I *have* been patient. I didn't say a word when Harris took me away, for no good reason, from the place where everybody was kind to me. I had paid him every cent of my earnings. They all thought I was an excellent worker."

"I know, but Harris *is* your master."

"By what right? None! I'm a better man than he is. I know more about business. I'm a better manager. I can read and write better. And I've learned everything on my own. What right does he have to make me do work that any horse could do? He wants to bring me down, so he gives me the meanest, dirtiest tasks. He continually insults and torments me. I had hoped to do my work and have some time left for reading, but the more I do, the more he loads on. He says I have the devil in me. One of these days it will come out in a way that he won't like."

"Don't talk like that, George. You have to be careful."

"Just yesterday, as I was loading stones into a cart, his son Richard stood there, slashing his whip so near the horse that the creature was frightened. As pleasantly as I could, I asked him to stop. He kept on. I asked him again. Then he began striking me. I stopped him by grabbing his arm. He screamed and kicked and ran to his father and told him that I was fighting him. Harris came in a rage and said he'd teach me who was master. He tied me to a tree, cut switches for Richard, and told him he could whip me until he was tired. And Richard did. Some day I'll make Harris pay for it." George's eyes burned with anger.

"I always thought I should obey my master and mistress," Eliza said gently.

"Well, the Shelbys have treated you decently. They've fed you, clothed you, and given you a good education. But I've been cursed, slapped, kicked, and whipped. I've paid for my keeping a hundred times over. My only comfort was poor little Carlo. He slept with me at night and followed me around during the day. He always looked at me as if he understood how I felt. The other day I was feeding him a few scraps I had picked up by the kitchen door and Harris came along. He said that I was feeding Carlo at his expense and that he couldn't afford to have every nigger keeping a dog. He ordered me to tie a stone to Carlo's neck and throw him into the pond."

"Oh, George, you didn't do it!"

"Of course not. I was flogged for refusing to. Then Harris did it. He and Richard pelted Carlo with stones as he drowned. Carlo looked at me the whole time, wondering why I didn't save him."

"Oh, George. Trust in God, and things will get better."

"I'm not a Christian like you, Eliza. My heart is full of bitterness. I don't believe in God. Why would God let things be the way they are?"

"We must have faith. Mistress says that when everything goes wrong, we have to believe that everything is for the best."

"That's easy for rich white people to say. Lately Harris has been saying that he was a fool to let me marry you. He says he won't let me come here anymore. He says I have to marry his slave Mina and live in a cabin with her. Otherwise he'll sell me down river."

"But we were married by a minister!" Eliza exclaimed.

"That doesn't matter. The law doesn't recognize marriages between slaves. If Harris chooses to part us, he can." Eliza paled. "I'm leaving, Eliza. I'm going to Canada."

"Canada!"

"When I'm there, I'll earn money to buy you and Harry," George said. "That's the best we can hope for. Shelby is kind. He won't refuse to sell you and Harry to me."

"What if you're captured?" Eliza asked.

"I'll kill myself before I let that happen. I'll be free or die."

"Oh, George, don't lay hands on yourself or anyone else! How will you escape?"

"I've made some preparations, and some people are going to help me. In about a week you'll hear that I'm missing. Goodbye for now," George said, holding Eliza's hands and gazing into her eyes. They stood silent. Then, weeping, they parted.

CHAPTER 5

The cabin of Tom, Chloe, and their children was a small log building close to the Shelbys' house. In front of the cabin was a small garden where a variety of fruits and vegetables flourished, each summer, under careful tending. Also in summer, marigolds, petunias, and other flowers—Chloe's delight and pride—unfolded their splendors.

Inside, a bed covered with a white spread stood in one corner. Beside it lay a large piece of carpet. This corner was off-limits to children. A crude little trundle bed stood in another corner. A portrait of George Washington and brightly colored pictures of Biblical scenes adorned the wall over the fireplace.

Chloe was cooking meat and vegetables in a pot over the fire. She was plump, with a round, shiny black face under a well-starched checked turban. Chloe's stuffed and roasted chicken, turkey, and duck were considered the best around, as were her cornbread and corn muffins. It was Chloe who prepared dinners for the Shelbys' guests.

In one corner Tom and Chloe's young sons, Mose and Pete, cheered on their baby sister, Polly, as she attempted to walk. All three children had glistening black eyes and fat, shining cheeks. Polly repeatedly rose to her feet, balanced a moment, then tumbled down.

A rickety table stood in front of the fire. It was covered with a cloth and set with brightly decorated cups and saucers. Tom, Shelby's best farmhand, was seated at the table. He was a large, broad-chested, powerful man. His skin was glossy black. His features displayed seriousness, intelligence, and kindness. His manner was self-respecting and dignified.

With a pencil Tom was carefully and slowly copying letters onto a piece of slate while James Shelby, a bright boy of fifteen, looked on as instructor. "Not that way, Uncle Tom," James said as Tom curved the tail of g in the wrong direction. "That makes q instead." James quickly wrote a g and a q for Tom to compare. Tom patiently tried again.

Chloe was greasing a griddle with a scrap of bacon on a fork. "Aunt Chloe, I'm getting mighty hungry," James said. "Is the cake almost done?"

"I'll check, Master James," Chloe said, lifting

the lid of the bake kettle and examining the pound cake inside. "It's a lovely brown. Master James, sit down with Tom. I'll take up the sausages and have the first batch of pancakes on your plates in no time." Chloe heaped pancakes onto James's plate and then turned back to the griddle.

"Now for the cake," James said after he'd eaten the pancakes.

Chloe sliced the cake. "Eat away. You won't get anything to beat that."

Speaking with his mouth full, James said, "Ray Burton says that their Ginny is a better cook than you."

"Those Burtons don't know what they're talking about!" Chloe said indignantly. "They don't have half the style of Master and Mistress. Ginny's alright with plain, common cooking, but she can't do anything fancy, the way I can."

"Don't worry, Aunt Chloe, I'd take your puddings and pies over anyone else's any day," James said. As James ate, Mose and Pete watched hungrily from the opposite corner. "Here, Mose, Pete," James said, breaking off chunks and throwing them at the children. "You want some, don't you? Aunt Chloe, make them some pancakes."

Having eaten their fill, Tom and James moved to comfortable seats in the chimney corner while Chloe, after baking a pile of pancakes, took Polly onto her lap and began alternately filling Polly's mouth and her own. She also distributed pancakes to Mose and Pete, who ate them while rolling around on the floor under the table, tickling each other, and occasionally pulling Polly's toes.

When Mose and Pete finished eating, they emerged from under the table and, with molasses on their hands and faces, kissed Polly. "Get along with you!" Chloe said, pushing them away. "Go to the spring and wash yourselves." Laughing, Mose and Pete hurried out of doors, where they screamed with merriment.

Chloe poured some water from a cracked teapot onto an old towel and began rubbing the molasses from Polly's face and hands. Then she set Polly in Tom's lap and started clearing away supper. Polly pulled Tom's nose, fingered his face, and buried her fat hands in his thick hair. "Isn't she pretty?" Tom said, holding Polly at arm's length to get a full view. Getting up, he set Polly on his broad shoulder and began to dance.

When Mose and Pete returned, Chloe said, "Time for the prayer meeting! Master James, will you stay and read for us?" Pleased to be the center of attention, James readily agreed.

The room soon filled with a mixed assembly of slaves, from a fifteen-year-old girl to an eighty-year-old man. A few of the worshippers belonged to families who lived nearby. People gossiped about where Aunt Sally got her new red kerchief, how Master was thinking of buying a new colt, and how "Mistress is going to give Eliza the polka-dot muslin dress." After a while the gathering began to sing hymns, which ranged from solemn to wildly exuberant. As they sang, some laughed, some cried, some clapped, and some shook hands with one other. By request, James read the last chapters of Revelation. He often was interrupted by exclamations such as "Praise the Lord!" Many regarded Tom as a sort of minister because he was so pious. When he prayed, it was with moving earnestness. Tom led the group in prayer.

CHAPTER 6

Daniel Haley and Arthur Shelby sat in the Shelbys' dining room, at a table covered with papers and writing implements. Shelby counted out bills and pushed them over to Haley, who also counted them. "Now for the signing," Haley said. Shelby drew the bills of sale toward him and hurriedly signed them, wanting to finish with the disagreeable business. Haley took a parchment out of a worn valise, looked it over for a moment, and handed it to Shelby, who took it with a gesture of suppressed eagerness. "That's it, then," Haley said, getting up.

"Yes," Shelby said with a sigh.

"You don't seem pleased," Haley said.

"Haley, don't forget that you've promised not to sell Tom without knowing what sort of hands he's going into."

"You've just done that yourself," Haley said.

"Circumstances forced me to," Shelby said.

"Well, they might force *me* to as well," Haley

24

said. "However, I'll try to get Tom a good master." Haley left, and Shelby smoked a cigar.

That night in the Shelbys' bedroom, Arthur lounged in an easy chair, looking over some letters that had come in the afternoon mail. Margaret sat before her mirror, brushing out the complicated braids and curls in which Eliza had arranged her hair. Margaret had excused Eliza's attendance that night and sent her to bed. Turning to her husband, Margaret said, "By the way, Arthur, who was that low-bred man you dined with today?"

"Daniel Haley," Arthur said, turning uneasily in his chair.

"Haley? Who is he? What business does he have with us?"

"I did some business with him the last time I was in Mississippi."

"He felt entitled to call on you and dine here?" Margaret said.

"I invited him. We had some business to attend to."

"Is he a slave trader?" Margaret asked. "Eliza said that you were talking with a trader. She was afraid you might sell Harry." Margaret continued to brush her hair. "I told her you never would sell any of our people."

"Well, Margaret, that's what I've always said and felt. But the fact is, I need to sell some of them."

"To that creature? Impossible! Arthur, you can't be serious."

"I've agreed to sell Tom," Arthur said.

"What! Our Tom? That good, faithful creature? He's been your faithful servant from boyhood. Oh, Arthur! And you promised him his freedom! You and I have spoken to him about it a hundred times. I can believe anything now! I can believe that you even could sell little Harry!"

"I *have*. I've agreed to sell Tom and Harry," Arthur said.

"Oh, my God!" Margaret exclaimed.

"I don't know why you act as if I'm some kind of monster. People sell their slaves every day."

"Why Tom and Harry?" Margaret asked.

"They brought the highest sum. If you wish, I can sell Eliza instead. Haley made me a large offer for her."

"That scoundrel!"

"I didn't agree, out of regard for your feelings," Arthur said.

"Arthur, you must allow me to intercede for these poor creatures. Although he's a Negro, Tom is a noble, faithful fellow. I think he would lay down his life for you."

"I believe that he *would*. But what's the use of this conversation? It's done."

"Sacrifice the money, then. Oh, Arthur, I've tried to do my duty to these poor, simple creatures. I've cared for them, instructed them, and watched over them for years. I know all their little cares and joys. How can I ever again hold up my head among them if we sell as faithful, good, and trusting a creature as poor Tom? How can we violate all that we've taught our people to love and value? I've taught them the duties of parent and child, husband and wife. How can we now show that we value money more than any duty, any relation, however sacred? I've preached to Eliza about the duties of a Christian mother. How can we turn around and sell her only child?"

"I'm sorry you feel this way, Margaret, but I had no choice. I was in debt to Haley. If I hadn't paid up, we would have lost the farm. Then, we would have had to sell more slaves than just Tom and Harry. Haley wanted the child. I had to agree."

"This is what comes of owning slaves!" Margaret cried. "It's an evil practice! I've never been comfortable with it!"

"Wise and pious men disagree with you. Reverend Brook doesn't think slavery is evil. Just last Sunday his sermon..."

"I don't want to hear any of his sermons ever again!"

"I've done the best that circumstances would allow," Arthur said.

Margaret fingered her gold watch and said

desperately, "Won't this watch do something? It was expensive. Let me at least save Eliza's child."

"No, Margaret. I'm sorry you're reacting this way. The bills of sale already are signed and in Haley's hands. I was in his power, and he's a hard man. He doesn't care about anything but profit. He'd sell his own mother."

"And that man now owns Tom and Harry!"

"He takes possession tomorrow. You'd better arrange a drive somewhere with Eliza, so she won't be here when Haley takes Harry."

"No! I won't be your accomplice in this despicable business. God forgive us!"

From inside a large closet just outside the bedroom, Eliza had listened to the whole conversation. Pale and trembling, she now hurried into her room. Harry lay sleeping on the bed, his rosy mouth half open, his fat little hands lying on the bedcovers.

Eliza took a pencil and piece of paper and hastily wrote, "Dear Mistress, don't think me ungrateful. I heard everything that you and Master said tonight. I'm going to try to save Harry. You can't blame me. God bless and reward you for all your kindness."

Eliza went to a drawer and made up a little package of clothing for Harry, adding his favorite toy. With a handkerchief, she tied the package around her waist. Then she put on her shawl and bonnet.

Eliza woke Harry. "Where are we going, Mother?" he asked as Eliza dressed him in his little coat and cap.

"Hush, Harry. No one must hear us. We have to go away," Eliza whispered. She took Harry in her arms, opened the door onto the veranda, and glided out. It was a frosty, starlit night. Eliza wrapped her shawl around Harry, who clung to her neck. Bruno the dog, who slept at the end of the porch, rose with a low growl as Eliza approached. Eliza gently said his name, and Bruno, an old pet and playmate of hers, wagged his tail. Eliza glided forward to the window of Tom and Chloe's cabin. She tapped lightly on the windowpane.

"Good Lord! What's that?" Chloe said, starting up and pushing the curtain aside. "It's Eliza!" Tom hurriedly lit a candle. Holding it, Chloe opened the door. The candle's light fell on Eliza's haggard face and wild eyes. "My God, Eliza. What's happened?" Chloe asked.

"I'm running away. Master sold Harry!"

"Sold him?" Tom and Chloe echoed in disbelief.

"Yes. To a slave trader. He sold you too, Uncle Tom. Come daylight, the man will be here to take possession."

Tom's eyes widened with fear and amazement. He collapsed into his chair. "God have pity on us!" Chloe said. "Is it really possible?"

"Master didn't want to sell, and Mistress pleaded and begged for us, but he told her the deal was done. He owed the trader money. If he hadn't paid up, he would have lost the farm, and *more* people would have ended up being sold."

"You have to go with Eliza, Tom!" Chloe said. "You can't be toted down river, where they kill niggers with hard work and starvation. I'd rather die than go there. Hurry now. Get ready."

Sorrowfully and quietly Tom said, "No. I'm not going. If I run away, Master might have to sell someone else. I guess I can bear it as well as anyone. It's right for Eliza to go for Harry's sake, but..." Tom now looked at his own children and started to sob.

"I saw George this afternoon," Eliza said to Chloe. "Harris has pushed him beyond breaking point. He's going to run away to Canada. If you can, please get word to him. Tell him why I went and that I'll try to get to Canada. Give him my love. Tell him that if we can't meet in Canada"— her voice caught—"we'll meet someday in heaven." After some final words and tears, Eliza, clasping her frightened child in her arms, hurried away.

CHAPTER 7

Because they had gone to bed late and had slept unsoundly, Margaret and Arthur slept late the next morning. After pulling her bell three times for Eliza and getting no response, Margaret said, "I wonder what's keeping Eliza."

Arthur stood in front of his mirror, sharpening his razor. The door opened, and a young black man entered with Arthur's shaving water. "Andy," Margaret said, "tell Eliza that I've rung for her three times."

Andy soon returned, his eyes wide with astonishment. "Lord, Mistress. Eliza's drawers all are open, and her things are lying every which way. I think she's cleared out!"

Arthur exclaimed, "She found out, and she's run off!"

"Thank God!" Margaret said.

"You talk like a fool, Margaret. This could cause me considerable trouble. Haley saw that I hesitated about selling Harry. He'll think I arranged this." Arthur hastily left the room.

When Haley, booted and spurred, entered the Shelbys' parlor, Arthur said, "Andy, take Mr. Haley's hat and riding whip. Please take a seat, sir. I regret to say that the child you purchased no longer is here. His mother overheard that her child was sold. She has taken him and run off in the night."

"What? I expected fair dealing, Shelby!" Haley fumed.

"What, sir, am I to understand by that remark?" Threatening a duel, Shelby said, "If any man calls my honor into question, I have only one answer for him."

Haley cowered. In a softer voice he complained, "It's mighty hard on a fellow to lose out this way."

"Mr. Haley, I acknowledge that you have cause for disappointment. However, I have had nothing to do with the disappearance of this woman and her child. I will provide horses and servants and otherwise assist you to recover your property."

"Do you have any dogs for tracking niggers?" Haley asked.

"No." After a pause, Arthur said, "If you would like some breakfast, please take some."

In both the house and the fields, all the slaves spoke of Eliza's flight. Andy told another slave, Sam, to ready the horses Bill and Jerry. "You and I have to go with Mr. Haley to find Eliza."

"I'm the nigger for the job!" Sam said proudly. "See if I don't catch her."

"Mistress doesn't want her caught," Andy said.

Sam's eyes widened. "How do you know that?"

"I heard her say so."

Sam scratched his head in puzzlement. "I would've thought that Mistress would scour the whole world in search of Eliza."

"She doesn't want Haley to get Harry," Andy said. "Get the horses ready."

Sam brought Bill and Jerry up to the house. Haley's horse, a skittish white colt, stood nearby. Sam picked up a small, sharp triangular beechnut and slipped it under the colt's saddle, so that the least weight on the saddle would irritate the colt.

Margaret appeared on the balcony and beckoned to Sam. "Sam, you and Andy are to go with Mr. Haley to show him the road and help him. Be careful of the horses. Jerry was a little lame last week. Don't ride him too fast," Margaret said with emphasis.

"Yes, Mistress," Sam said. Then he told Andy about the beechnut he'd placed under the colt's saddle. "When the colt starts to act up, we'll let go of Bill and Jerry as if to help Mr. Haley. Then Bill and Jerry will run off. That will delay things." Sam and Andy chuckled.

Haley appeared on the veranda. "Look alive,

boys," he said to Sam and Andy. "We mustn't lose any time."

Sam gave Haley his reins and held his stirrup while Andy untied Bill and Jerry. The instant Haley touched the saddle, the colt bounded up and threw Haley off onto some soft turf, then pranced away toward the lower end of the lawn. Bill and Jerry, whom Andy had let loose, followed the colt. To increase the confusion, Sam and Andy ran around shouting.

Haley's colt kept avoiding his pursuers. As soon as they would come almost within reach of him, he would whisk off with a snort and career far down some alley of the woodlot. Haley ran up and down, cursed, and stamped. Arthur vainly shouted directions from the balcony. Looking out of her bedroom window, Margaret laughed, suspecting the cause of the confusion.

Three hours later, about noon, Sam was mounted on Jerry. The colt was by his side, reeking with sweat. The colt's flashing eyes and dilated nostrils showed that the spirit of freedom hadn't entirely subsided. Haley was furious. "Let's get started!" he growled.

"Mr. Haley," Sam said in a humble tone, "we're all ready to drop, and the horses are all sweaty. They need to be rubbed down. I guess we can't start now until after dinner. We can catch up with Eliza. She never was much of a walker."

Having overheard this conversation from the

veranda, Margaret resolved to do her part. She came forward and, courteously expressing concern about Haley's accident, pressed him to stay for dinner, saying that the cook would bring it to the table immediately.

Haley went to the parlor while Sam and Andy went to the stable with the horses. "Did you see him fuming, Andy? Did you hear him swearing?" Sam said. The two had a good laugh.

Tom was summoned to the parlor, where Arthur Shelby said, "Tom, this is Mr. Haley. He's your new owner. Today he has other business to attend to, but he'll be taking you away soon."

Tom stood very straight. "Master, I was just eight years old, and you were one year old, when your mother put you into my arms. She said, 'There, Tom. He's your young master. Take good care of him.' I've never broken any promise to your mother or you."

"God knows you speak the truth," Arthur said. "If I could help it, no one on earth would buy you."

"I'll buy you back as soon as I can," Margaret said. "Sir," she said to Haley, "let me know who buys him."

"I might bring him back myself in a year and sell him back to you," Haley said.

CHAPTER 8

Eliza was desolate when she turned from Tom and Chloe's cabin. She was leaving the only home she ever had known. But her fear was greater than her sadness. Pressing Harry to her chest, she hurried forward. The frosty ground crackled beneath her feet. Every sound and fluttering shadow increased her fear. Eliza quickly passed the boundaries of the farm, the grove, and the woodlot.

With his arms around Eliza's neck, Harry slept. Daylight found Eliza and Harry many miles from all familiar objects, on an open highway. Eliza planned to escape across the Ohio River to Ohio, where slavery was illegal. When horses and vehicles began to move along the highway, Eliza realized that her hurried pace and desperate manner would attract suspicion, so she put Harry down, adjusted her dress and bonnet, and walked on as rapidly as she could without looking as if she were fleeing.

After a while, Eliza and Harry came to a thick patch of woodland with a clear brook. Harry complained of hunger and thirst. Eliza took Harry behind a large rock that concealed them from the road and gave him breakfast out of her package. Harry wondered and grieved that his mother didn't eat. He tried to push some of his cake into her mouth. "No, no, darling," Eliza said. "Mother can't eat until you're safe." As soon as Harry finished eating, Eliza and Harry resumed their walk down the road. Eliza rejoiced that their light skin made them less likely to attract notice.

At noon Eliza stopped at a neat farmhouse to rest and buy some food. A friendly woman accepted Eliza's statement that she was traveling to visit friends. An hour before sunset, Eliza, tired and footsore, entered a village along the swollen and turbulent Ohio River. Great chunks of ice floated in the river. This ice, Eliza realized, would prevent the ferry from running. She turned into a small inn to inquire. The hostess was stirring a stew over the fire.

"Is there any ferry or boat to take people across the river?" Eliza asked.

"No," the hostess said. "The boats have stopped running."

Eliza's look of dismay struck the woman, who asked, "You're anxious to cross over? Is anyone sick?"

"I walked far with my child today, expecting to take the ferry," Eliza said.

"Maybe I can help you. Solomon!" the hostess called from the window toward a small back building. A man in a leather apron appeared at the door. "Sol, is that man going to tote the barrels over tonight?"

"He said he'd try," Solomon answered.

Turning back to Eliza, the hostess said, "A man probably is going over with some barrels tonight. He'll be here for supper. Why don't you sit down and wait for him?" She offered Harry a cake, but he cried with exhaustion.

"He isn't used to walking, and I've hurried him," Eliza said.

"Bring him into this room," the hostess said, opening the door to a small bedroom with a comfortable bed.

Eliza laid Harry on the bed and held his hands in hers until he slept. Too fearful to sleep, she gazed longingly at the surging water between her and freedom.

CHAPTER 9

Although Margaret Shelby had said that dinner was about to be served, it didn't appear. Chloe intentionally prepared everything more slowly than usual. One boy purposely overturned the gravy dish; then more gravy had to be prepared. Another boy fell while carrying the water pitcher, so he had to go to the spring for more. Meanwhile, Haley squirmed and paced with impatience.

Finally dinner was served. At two o'clock Sam and Andy brought the horses up to the hitching posts. Haley asked Sam, "What's the fastest way to the river?"

"There are two roads: a dirt road and the highway," Sam said. "Eliza would take the dirt road because it's less traveled," he lied.

"Alright," Haley said. "Which way?"

Sam indicated the rough road, and Haley plunged into it, followed by Sam and Andy. The road had once been a thoroughfare to the Ohio

River, but it had been abandoned many years before, after the laying of the highway. The road was clear for about an hour's ride. After that, farms and fences cut across it. Sam knew this. After riding for about an hour, the group encountered a barn standing across the road. "You rascal!" Haley fumed at Sam. "You knew about this!"

"I didn't," Sam lied. "I knew that this road wasn't well traveled, and I told you that." The three turned around and headed for the highway.

About an hour after Eliza had laid Harry to sleep in the village inn, Haley, Sam, and Andy rode into the same place. Eliza was standing by the window, looking out in another direction, when Sam spotted her. Haley and Andy were two yards behind. Sam pretended that his hat blew off, so that he could utter a cry that alerted Eliza. She drew back.

Eliza's room opened by a side door to the river. She grabbed Harry and sprang toward this door. Haley saw her just as she was disappearing down the bank. Jumping from his horse and calling loudly on Sam and Andy, Haley was after her like a hound after a deer. In a moment Eliza was at the river's edge. Haley was right behind. Eliza leaped onto an ice floe. The danger and daring of this action made Sam, Andy, and even Haley cry out. The huge chunk of ice on which Eliza landed creaked under her. With desperate energy, she leaped to another, then another. She slipped and stumbled, springing up again. Her shoes were gone. Her stockings were cut from her feet. Blood marked every step. Then, as in a dream, she reached the Ohio side.

A man helped her up the bank. "By God, you're a brave gal!" he said.

"My child has been sold!" Eliza cried. Pointing to Haley on the Kentucky shore, she said, "That man is his new owner. Please help me!"

"Go there!" the man said, pointing to a large white house off the village's main street. "They're kind folks. They'll help you."

"God bless you!" Eliza said.

"You've earned your freedom, and I, for one, won't take it from you."

Clasping Harry to her chest, Eliza walked away firmly and swiftly. Haley had watched in amazement. He now turned an inquiring look on Sam and Andy. "I hope you'll excuse us from trying *that* road," Sam said with a chuckle.

"You laugh!" Haley growled, striking at Sam's head with his riding whip. Sam successfully ducked. He and Andy ran up the bank, jumped onto their horses, and galloped home.

Haley went inside the inn. The hostess showed him where Eliza and Harry had rested. Eliza's shawl was on the bed. Haley took the shawl and then went to the main room for a drink.

Ted Loker, a tall, broad, muscular man, soon entered. He wore a coat of buffalo hide, with the hair outward, that contributed to his fierce appearance. His face showed brutality. Loker was accompanied by Stephen Marks, a short, slender man whose motions were cat-like. Marks had keen black eyes; a long, thin nose; thin lips; a sharp chin; and thin, sleek black hair. Loker half filled a big tumbler with whiskey and gulped it down. In a thin, quivering voice, Marks ordered a mint julep, which he drank in sips.

"Ted!" Haley exclaimed, coming forward and extending his hand to Loker.

"The devil!" Loker responded. "What brings you here, Haley?"

Marks stopped sipping and shrewdly observed Haley.

"I say, Ted, this meeting is lucky," Haley said. "I have a problem that you can help me with."

"So, that's why you're glad to see me," Loker said.

Ignoring the insult, Haley asked, "Is this your partner?"

"Yes. Marks, this is Dan Haley. He used to be my partner in Mississippi."

"Pleased to meet you," Marks said, extending a long, thin hand.

"My treat, gentlemen," Haley said. Turning to the bartender, he said, "Bring us hot water, sugar, cigars, and plenty of liquor."

When the three were seated around a table indulging themselves, Haley recited his troubles. The story of Eliza's escape amused Marks, who said, "Shelby and his niggers took *you*, didn't they? Too bad we can't breed gals who don't care about their babies."

"Babies are a nuisance. You'd think they'd be glad to be rid of them," Haley said.

"I bought a gal once who had a sickly child with a crooked back," Marks said. "I gave the child away. I thought the mother would be glad to be rid of him, but you should've seen the way she carried on."

"Last summer I swapped a blind child for a keg of whiskey," Haley said. "When I went to take him from his mother, she jumped into the river with him. They went down and never came back up."

"When I buy a child," Loker said with contempt, "I just put my fist to the mother's face and say 'One word out of you, and I'll smash your face in. This young one is mine, not yours.' That shuts them up. What's your business, Haley? You want us to catch this gal?"

"I don't care about the gal. She belongs to Shelby. It's the boy I want. I paid for him."

"What's the gal like?" Marks asked.

"White, beautiful, and well brought up. I'd have given Shelby a thousand for her and still made a hefty profit when I sold her."

"How about this, then?" Marks said to both Haley and Loker. "Ted and I do the catching, the boy goes to Dan, and Ted and I take the gal to New Orleans. I'll pretend to be her owner."

Loker brought his heavy fist down on the table. "We'll do it! But, Haley, you've got to hand over fifty dollars right now. Otherwise we might try to catch them, fail, and come away with nothing. If I find the boy, I'll bring him to Cincinnati and leave him at Granny Belcher's on the landing."

"Let's get to particulars," Marks said. "Dan, you saw this gal when she landed?"

"As plainly as I see you."

"A man helped her up the bank?" Marks continued.

"Yes," Haley said.

"Most likely, someone has taken her in. What do you think, Ted?" Marks said.

"We must cross the river tonight," Loker said.

"There's no boat," Marks said.

"I heard the hostess say that a man is going to boat across this evening. We have to go with him," Loker said.

"You've got good dogs?" Haley asked.

"First-rate," Marks said, "but you don't have anything of the runaway's to give them the scent."

"Yes, I do," Haley said. "Here's her shawl. She left it on the bed."

"Give it here," Loker said.

"On second thought, the dogs might damage the gal," Haley said.

"That's a consideration," Marks said. "Our dogs tore one fellow half to pieces before we could get them off."

"That won't do because she's to be sold for her looks," Haley said.

"Yes," Marks agreed. "We won't use the dogs."

When the man came with the boat, Haley reluctantly gave Loker fifty dollars, and Marks and Loker went their way.

Between ten and eleven, Sam and Andy arrived home. Margaret Shelby flew to the balcony. "Is that you, Sam? Where's Eliza?"

"She made it across the Ohio River," Sam answered.

"Thank God!" Margaret exclaimed.

CHAPTER 10

The light of a cheerful fire shone on the carpet of a cozy parlor and glittered on teacups and a bright teapot. U.S. senator John Bird of Ohio removed his boots and put on handsome new slippers that his wife, Mary, had knit for him while he was away in Washington, D.C.

Mary was happily supervising the table arrangements, periodically issuing warnings to her two young sons. "Davey, leave the doorknob alone. Scott, don't climb on the table." Turning to her husband, Mary said, "My dear, it's so good to have you here."

"It's good to *be* here—much better than listening to all those boring Senate speeches."

"What has the Senate been doing?"

"Not much of importance."

"Is it true that Congress has passed a law forbidding people from helping runaway slaves?"

"Yes. Slaveholders in Kentucky and other states are upset because a lot of that has been going on."

"It's illegal to give those poor creatures something to eat and some old clothes, shelter them for a night, and send them quietly on their way?" Mary asked.

"Yes, it's illegal," John said.

Mary was a short, timid woman with mild blue eyes, a peach complexion, and a sweet voice. Her husband and sons were nearly her entire world. Usually she influenced her family by pleading and persuading rather than by arguing or commanding. But any form of cruelty threw her into a passion. Generally the most indulgent mother, she had reacted with fury when she once found her boys stoning a kitten. She had spanked them long and hard, sent them to bed without supper, and then wept. Never again had her boys abused an animal.

On the present occasion, Mary reddened, rose quickly, walked up to her husband, and said in a determined tone, "Do you think such a law is right?"

"Yes, Mary, I do," John said.

"I never would have believed it of you. You didn't vote for it, did you?"

"Yes, I did," John said.

"You should be ashamed of yourself! It's a wicked law. I'll break it the first chance I get. What have things come to if a person can't give a warm supper and a bed to poor, starving creatures who have been oppressed all their lives?"

"I appreciate your feelings, my dear, and I love you for them. But we mustn't let our feelings interfere with our judgment. We have to prevent public unrest."

"Rubbish! Would you turn away a poor, shivering, hungry creature because they're a runaway? Would you put them in jail?"

With discomfort John answered, "It would be a painful duty."

"Duty! Our first duty is to be good Christians!" Mary declared.

At this point Cudjoe, an elderly black servant, put his head in at the door and asked "Mistress" to come into the kitchen. Relieved, John sat down in an armchair and began to read the newspaper.

"John, come here!" Mary called from the kitchen. Upon entering the kitchen, John gasped at the sight of Eliza, who had fainted into a chair. Mary and a middle-aged black servant named Sarah were trying to restore Eliza while Cudjoe had Harry on his knee and was pulling off the child's shoes and socks and rubbing his cold little feet.

"She's a sight to behold," Sarah said compassionately. "She came in, asked if she could warm herself a bit, and then fainted."

"Poor woman!" Mary said.

Eliza slowly opened her eyes. She sprang up crying, "Where's Harry? Have they taken him?"

Harry jumped from Cudjoe's knee, ran to his mother, and cried, "Here I am, Mother!"

"Oh, Ma'am," Eliza pleaded to Mary, "please protect us! Don't let them get him!"

"No one here will hurt you," Mary said reassuringly. "You're safe. Don't be afraid."

"God bless you!" Eliza said. Covering her face, she sobbed. Harry hugged his mother.

Tears came into Mary's eyes. "Where did you come from?" she gently asked. "What do you need?"

Mary's tone calmed Eliza, who answered, "I came from Kentucky."

"When?" John asked.

"Tonight."

"How did you get here?" he asked.

"I crossed the river on foot by jumping over the ice."

"Crossed on foot!" a number of people exclaimed.

"Yes," Eliza said. "I jumped over the ice because my pursuers were right behind me. There was no other way."

"Lord, Mistress," Cudjoe said to Mary, "the ice is all broken up in blocks swinging and teetering up and down the water."

"Were you a slave?" John asked.

"Yes, sir. I belonged to a man in Kentucky."

"Was he unkind to you?" John asked.

"No. He was a good master," Eliza said.

"Was your mistress unkind to you?" John continued.

"No. My mistress always was good to me."

"Why did you leave, then?"

Eliza looked at Mary and noticed that she was dressed in mourning. "Ma'am, have you lost a child?"

The question opened a wound. Only a month before, Mary's youngest son had died. John turned around and walked to the window. Mary burst into tears. Recovering her voice, she said, "Yes."

"Then, you'll feel for me," Eliza said. "Harry is my only child. I've never slept apart from him. He's my comfort and pride. They were going to take him away from me. They sold him to a slave trader who was going to take him south. When I found out that he'd been sold, I took him and ran off in the night. The slave trader and two of my master's slaves came after me. They were right behind me, so I jumped onto the ice. Somehow I got across, and a man helped me up the bank."

"You said you had a kind master!" John said indignantly.

"He owed the trader money. He paid his debt by selling Harry and a man named Tom."

"Do you have a husband?" John asked.

"Yes. His name is George. He belongs to another man. His master is cruel and hardly ever allowed George to come see me. He's threatened to sell George down south."

"Where will you go?" Mary asked.

"To Canada. Is it far?"

"Poor child, it *is* far," Mary said, "but we'll see what can be done for you. Sarah, make her up a bed in your room." Eliza soon fell asleep with her arm around Harry.

In the parlor Mary sat thinking, swaying in her rocking chair before the fire. John paced. "Do you think any of your dresses would fit her?" he asked. "No, I guess she's too large, isn't she?"

A slight smile appeared on Mary's face. "We'll see."

"What about that old cloak that you drape over me when I take my afternoon naps? You can give her that. She needs clothes," John said. Suddenly he stood motionless. "I say, Mary, she'll have to get away from here tonight. The trader will be after her bright and early tomorrow."

"Tonight! To where?"

Starting to put on his boots, John said, "I know where. My old client Nicholas van Trompe has come over from Kentucky and set all his slaves free. He's bought a place seven miles up the creek. It's back in the woods. Hardly anyone ever goes there. She'll be safe there. I'll have to take her myself."

"Why?" Mary asked.

"The creek has to be crossed twice," John said. "The second crossing is dangerous unless someone knows it as well as I do. I've crossed it a hundred times on horseback and know exactly the turns to take. So I have to take her myself. Cudjoe must hitch up the horses as quietly as possible about midnight. I'll take her to van Trompe's. Then Cudjoe must drive me to the next inn to take the stagecoach for Columbus that comes about three in the morning, so it will look as if I had the carriage for that."

Laying her hand on her husband's, Mary said with tears in her eyes, "Your heart is better than your head in this case, John. I couldn't love you if I didn't know you better than you know yourself."

Pleased with his wife's approval, John walked off to see about the carriage. At the door he stopped a moment, came back, and said with some hesitation, "Mary, I don't know how you'd feel about it, but there's a drawer full of things that were . . . Benny's. Maybe the boy could use them." He turned quickly and shut the door after him.

Mary opened the door to the little bedroom adjoining hers. She set a candle on a dresser and slowly opened one of the drawers. There were little coats, rows of small socks, even a pair of little shoes, worn and scuffed at the toes, as well as a toy horse and wagon, a top, a ball, and other toys. Mary sat down by the drawer and wept.

Then, with nervous haste, she began selecting the most practical items and gathered them into a bundle. Next she opened a wardrobe and removed two plain dresses. She sat down to her worktable and, with needle, scissors, and thimble, began letting them out as much as possible. She continued this until the clock in the corner struck midnight and she heard the low rattling of wheels at the door.

Coming in with his overcoat over his arm, John said, "Mary, you must wake her now. We have to go." Mary hurriedly put the items she had collected into a small, plain trunk, which she gave to John to place in the carriage.

Mary awakened Eliza and explained the plan. Eliza soon appeared at the door with Harry in her arms. She wore a cloak, bonnet, and shawl that had belonged to Mary. Mary hurried Eliza into the carriage. Eliza leaned out and extended her hand. Mary grasped it in her own. Eliza fixed her eyes on Mary's face and softly said, "God bless you." Then she fell back into the seat. The door was shut, and the carriage departed.

There had been a long period of rainy weather, so the road was muddy. A number of times the carriage stuck fast and Cudjoe and John had to get down and coax and pull the horses to strain forward until the carriage came loose.

It was far past midnight when the carriage arrived, dripping and bespattered, at the door of a large farmhouse. It took persistence to awaken the residents. At last, Nicholas van Trompe unlatched the door. He was over six feet tall. His thick, sand-colored hair was tousled. He had a beard of some days' growth.

"Hello, Nicholas," John said.

For a few minutes Nicholas stood holding a candle aloft and blinking at the travelers with a mystified expression. Then he exclaimed, "Senator Bird!"

"Will you shelter a poor woman and child from slave hunters?" John asked.

"I will," Nicholas said.

"Thank you," John said.

Opening the door wide, Nicholas led John and Eliza into the kitchen. Exhausted, Eliza dragged herself forward, with Harry sleeping in her arms. Nicholas held the candle to Eliza's face and, uttering a compassionate grunt, opened the door of a small bedroom and motioned for her to go in. "You have nothing to fear here," he told her. "I have seven sons, each six feet tall." Pointing to three rifles over the mantelpiece, he said, "If anyone comes, we'll be ready for them, so you just sleep now." He shut the door. "A beautiful woman," he said to John. "What's happened?"

John shared what he knew of Eliza's history. Nicholas was so moved that he wiped his eyes. He uncorked some bottled cider and offered it to

John. "You'd better stay here until daylight. My wife will have a bed ready for you in no time."

"Thank you, my good friend," John said, "but I have to go. I have to take the night coach to Columbus."

"Well, if you must, I'll show you a crossroad that will take you there better than the road you came on. That road's mighty bad." Nicholas got ready and, lantern in hand, soon guided John's carriage toward the desired road.

At the crossroad, John gave Nicholas a ten-dollar bill. "It's for her," he said.

"Certainly," Nicholas replied.

They shook hands and parted.

CHAPTER 11

It was a gray, drizzly morning that matched the downcast faces of those inside Tom and Chloe's cabin. An ironing cloth covered the small table before the fire. Fresh from the iron, a coarse but clean shirt hung on the back of a chair by the fire. Chloe had another shirt spread out before her on the table. She carefully ironed away every wrinkle, periodically raising her hand to her face to wipe away tears.

Tom sat near by, but neither he nor Chloe spoke. It was still early. The children lay asleep together in their little bed. Tom walked over to look at them. "It's the last time," he said.

Setting her iron down, Chloe sat down and wept. "I don't even know where you're going," she said. "Mistress says she'll try to buy you back in a year or two, but I don't think anybody who goes down river ever comes back. They work slaves to death on those plantations."

"The same God who is here will be there, Chloe," Tom said.

"Yes, but God lets dreadful things happen."

"I thank God that I'm the one who's been sold—not you or the children," Tom said.

"Master never should have let you be taken for his debts. He owed you your freedom and should have given it to you years ago. You've been completely faithful to him."

"He's still been a better master than most," Tom said.

"That may be, but it isn't right. But there's no use talking about it. It's done. I'll make you a good breakfast. Who knows when you'll get another?" Chloe gave Tom chicken, cornbread, and—a rare treat—preserves.

Bustling about after breakfast, Chloe said, "I'll gather all your clothes, although Haley probably will take all of them away. Who will take care of you if you're sick?" she asked, starting to cry again. Having awakened, Mose and Pete saw their mother crying and their father looking very sad. They, too, started to cry.

Following a light knocking, Chloe opened the door, and Margaret and James Shelby entered. Margaret looked pale and anxious. "Tom," she said. "We've come to say goodbye." Covering her face with her handkerchief, she began to sob.

James hurried up to Tom and threw his arms around him. "This is horrible, Uncle Tom!" he cried. "It's a mean, nasty shame. If I were a man, they wouldn't dare do it. I wouldn't let them!" He sobbed.

Tom stroked James's curly head with his large, strong hand and said tenderly, "I know you'll grow up to be a fine man, Master George."

"I will, Uncle Tom! I will!" the boy said passionately, still crying.

"Don't be discouraged," Tom said.

"When I'm a man, I'll come for you and bring you back," James said. "You'll be happy!" He broke off in sobs.

"Tom," Margaret said, "I can't give you anything that will do you any good. If I give you money, they'll just take it from you. But I swear before God that I'll keep track of you and bring you back as soon as I have enough money."

A kick opened the door. Having ridden hard the night before, Haley stood there in a foul mood. "Come on, nigger," he said to Tom. Taking off his hat to Margaret, he said, "Your servant, ma'am."

Furious, James said to Haley, "You watch how you speak to Uncle Tom!"

Chloe shut the box with Tom's things and wrapped string around it. She glared at Haley. Tom stood and took the heavy box onto his shoulder. Chloe took Polly in her arms and followed Tom to the wagon that stood before the Shelbys' house. Crying, Mose and Pete trailed behind.

A crowd of slaves had gathered around the wagon to say goodbye to Tom. Many of them were weeping. Haley strode through the crowd and told Tom, "Get in!" Tom got in, and Haley put a heavy pair of shackles around Tom's ankles. A gasp of indignation ran through the gathering.

"Mr. Haley, that precaution is entirely unnecessary," Margaret said.

"I don't know, ma'am," Haley said. "I've already lost the five hundred dollars I paid for the child. I'm not running any more risks."

Haley applied the whip to his horse. With a steady, mournful look fixed to the last on his family, Tom was driven away.

CHAPTER 12

After some time Haley said to Tom, "I'm going to gather a prime group to take down with you. We have to drive to Smithville. I'll put you in a jail there while I buy others." The thought of jail, which Tom associated with criminal behavior, alarmed and shamed him. He didn't say anything. By evening Haley and Tom reached Smithville. Haley went to a tavern and Tom to a jail.

About eleven o'clock the next morning, a crowd gathered around the courthouse steps. Some people smoked; others chewed tobacco and spat; still others swore or conversed. An auction was about to begin.

The people to be sold sat in a group apart, talking in low tones. One woman, named Hagar, was around fifty but looked older because of disease and years of hard work. She was partly blind and somewhat crippled with rheumatism. By her side stood her son Albert, a bright-looking boy of fourteen. All of Hagar's other children had been sold south. Hagar held on to Albert with both of her shaking hands and eyed with intense dread everyone who walked up to examine him. Jack, the oldest slave in the group, said to Hagar, "I spoke to Master Leonard about you. He thinks he might manage to sell you and Albert together."

Haley forced his way into the group. He walked up to Jack, pulled his mouth open, looked in, and felt his teeth. Haley made Jack stand straight, bend his back, and move in various ways to show his muscles. Then Haley passed on to the next man and put him through the same trial. Albert was next. Haley felt his arms, straightened his hands and looked at his fingers, and made him jump to show his agility.

"He won't be sold without me!" Hagar said passionately. "He and I go together. I'm still strong. I can do a lot of work."

"On a plantation?" Haley said with a contemptuous glance. "Not likely." Satisfied with his examination, he walked out of the group and stood with his hands in his pockets, his cigar in his mouth, and his hat cocked to one side.

"Clear the way!" the auctioneer called as he elbowed his way into the crowd. Hagar drew in her breath and clutched Albert. The bidding began. The men were quickly sold at prices that indicated brisk demand. Two of them went to

Haley. "Come on, young one," the auctioneer said to Albert, touching him with his gavel. "Stand up."

"Sell us together," Hagar begged, clutching Albert.

The auctioneer roughly pushed her away. "Come on, darky," he said to Albert, pushing him toward the auction block. Albert's fine figure and bright face raised an instant competition. Half a dozen bids were called out. Then the gavel fell. Haley had him.

Albert was pushed from the block toward his new owner, but he stopped and looked back at Hagar, who held out her shaking hands toward him. "Buy me too, Master," she begged Haley. "Buy me! I'll die if you don't!"

"You'll die if I *do*," Haley quipped. "That's the problem." He turned on his heels.

A man then bought Hagar for a trifle. The spectators began to disperse. Hagar wailed with grief as she was led to the wagon of her new master.

Haley pushed his three purchases together, handcuffed their wrists, and fastened each handcuff to a long chain. Then he drove them before him to the jail.

A few days later Haley and his new purchases were on a steamboat. Enjoying the beautiful weather, he strolled the upper deck, along with many ladies and gentlemen. His possessions were below, stored with other freight. Sitting in a knot, they talked quietly. Laying his chained hand on Tom's knee, the article designated "Nathan, aged thirty" said, "My wife doesn't know anything about this."

"Where does she live?" Tom asked.

"In an inn not far from here. I wish I could see her once more," Nathan said. The tears that fell as he spoke came as naturally as if he'd been white.

CHAPTER 13

Late in the afternoon of a drizzly day, the bar-room of a small inn in a Kentucky village was filled with large, tall hunters, all wearing hats. At each end of the fireplace sat a long-legged man with his chair tipped back and the heels of his muddy boots resting on the mantelpiece. Slaves bustled about. The fire crackled. The outer door and every window were wide open. The calico curtains flapped and snapped in a damp breeze.

Robert Wilson, George's former employer, entered with a valise and umbrella. After looking around, he retreated to the warmest corner, put his valise and umbrella under his chair, sat down, and glanced at the man sitting nearest him. This man spat out some tobacco juice and said, "How are you, stranger? I'm Ned Carter." Then he resumed chewing tobacco.

Wilson nodded courteously and said, "Robert Wilson." Some people were gathered around a large handbill. "What's that?" Wilson asked.

"Notice of a runaway," one of them answered. Then he read out loud:

> **My mulatto boy George has run away. He's six feet tall, very light, with curly brown hair. He's very intelligent. He speaks well and can read and write. He'll probably try to pass for a white man. His back and shoulders are deeply scarred. His right hand is branded with the letter H. I'll give $400 for him alive or for proof that he's been killed.**
>
> **Walter Harris**

Ned got up, came over to the handbill, and spat on it.

"Why did you do that?" the innkeeper asked.

"I'd do the same to the man who wrote it," Ned said. "Any man who treats his slave that way deserves to lose him."

"You're right, friend," Wilson said. "I know this boy. He used to work in my cloth factory. He was my best worker. He's a fine, smart fellow. He invented a machine for cleaning hemp, a valuable machine. It's gone into use in several factories. His master holds the patent."

"And makes plenty of money from it, I'm sure," Ned said. "But he turns around and brands the fellow. If I had the chance, I'd mark *him*."

"These smarter boys are always being saucy," a coarse-looking man said. "That's why they get whipped and branded."

"You mean, they insist on being men," Ned said dryly, "and that's unforgivable."

The approach of a one-horse buggy interrupted the discussion. Disguised as a wealthy Spanish-looking gentleman, George sat beside another runaway, Jim, who was driving. George had darkened his skin and dyed his hair black.

George walked in and, with a nod, indicated to a waiter where to place his trunk. He bowed to the company and, hat in hand, walked up to the bar and gave his name as Charles Butter. His aristocratic manner and looks impressed everyone in the inn. Jim pretended to be his slave. Turning, George sauntered up to the handbill and read it. "Jim," he said, "didn't we see a boy like this at Beman's?"

"Yes, Master," Jim said.

George asked the innkeeper for a private room in which to do some writing. While the room was being prepared, he sat on a chair in the middle of the main room and entered into conversation with the man who sat next to him.

Having recognized George, Wilson was alarmed. He walked up to George. "Mr. Wilson, I think," George said, extending his hand. "Forgive me for not recognizing you right away. I see you remember me."

"Ye . . . Yes, sir," Wilson said nervously.

A black boy announced that "Master's" room was ready.

"Jim, see to the trunks," George said. "Mr. Wilson, I'd like to have a few moments' conversation with you on business in my room, if you'd be so kind." Wilson followed George to a large upper chamber, where a newly made fire was crackling. George locked the door and, putting the key into his pocket, faced Wilson.

"George!" Wilson exclaimed.

"Yes," George said with a smile. "Some walnut bark has made my skin a genteel tan, and I've dyed my hair black, so I don't have the appearance described in the handbill."

"Oh, George! You're playing a dangerous game." Wilson paced nervously. "You've run away from your lawful master. I don't wonder at it, but you're breaking the law."

"The law!" George said bitterly. "What laws are there for slaves? We don't make the laws or consent to them."

"You're running an awful risk, George. If you're caught, it will be worse for you than ever. They'll half kill you and sell you down river."

"I know all this." George threw open his overcoat, revealing two pistols and a hunting knife. "I'm ready for them. I'll die rather than go down river. I was born because a white master raped a Negro slave." Wilson winced. "Yes, Mr. Wilson, that's the reality. But white people considered my father a gentleman and my good, honorable mother nothing but property. My mother's seven children were sold before her eyes, all to different masters. She kneeled before my new owner and begged him to buy her as well, so that she could be with me. He kicked her away with his heavy boot. When I was carted away, she screamed. I never saw her again. I grew up with no family at all, no one who loved me. When I met and married my wonderful wife, I scarcely could believe how happy I was. We have a beautiful son. But then Harris told me I must part from my wife and child and live with another woman. So I'm going to Canada, where I'll be allowed to be a man. I'll fight for my freedom to my last breath."

"Well, go ahead then, George, but be careful. Where's your wife?"

"She fled with our son in her arms. I don't know where. I pray to God that I'll find them." Wilson took a roll of bills from his pocketbook and offered them to George. "No, kind sir," George said. "I have enough money to get to Canada."

"Please take it, George! Money is a great help everywhere. You can't have too much of it. Please take it, my boy!"

"Very well," George said, "but I plan to repay you if I ever can." He took the money.

"Who is the Negro fellow who's with you?" Wilson asked.

"A brave and good fellow who went to Canada

more than a year ago. He's taking me to friends in Ohio who helped him. Then he's going to try to rescue his mother, who has a cruel master."

"It's very dangerous, George. If they catch you, they'll find the scar on your hand."

George drew off his glove and showed a newly healed scar. "Harris did that two weeks ago. I'll leave before daylight. I hope to sleep safely in Ohio by tomorrow night. They won't take me alive." George stood and extended his hand to Wilson. "Thank you, my good friend."

Wilson shook George's hand heartily, said "God be with you!" and left the room.

CHAPTER 14

Eliza swayed in a rocking chair in a Quaker home in Indiana. She was sewing by the fire in a large, neatly painted kitchen with a glossy yellow floor, neat stove, rows of shining pots and pans, and glossy green wood chairs. Harry gamboled across the floor.

Rachel Halliday sat by Eliza's side in a smaller rocking chair. She sorted dried peaches into a bright tin pan in her lap. Rachel wore typical Quaker clothes: a gray dress and shawl, white muslin handkerchief neatly folded across her chest, and white crepe cap. Her face was round and rosy. Her partially silver hair was parted smoothly back from a high placid forehead. Her brown eyes shone with kindness. As she rocked, her chair creaked and squeaked. "So you're thinking of going to Canada, Eliza?" Rachel asked.

"Yes, ma'am. I must go on."

"What will you do when you get there?"

Eliza's hands trembled, but she answered firmly, "I'll do anything I can find."

"You know you can stay here as long as you please," Rachel said.

"Oh, thank you, but I can't sleep at night. I'm always fearful that they'll take Harry. Last night I dreamed I saw the slave trader coming into the yard." Eliza shuddered.

"No runaway ever has been captured in our village. Try not to be afraid," Rachel said.

Isaac Halliday, a tall, straight, muscular man in a gray coat and pantaloons and a broad-rimmed hat, entered the kitchen.

"Any news?" Rachel asked.

"Peter Stebbins told me that they should be along tonight, with friends," Isaac said significantly.

"Indeed!" Rachel said, glancing at Eliza.

"Did you say your husband's name is George and his owner is Harris?" Isaac asked Eliza.

"Yes," Eliza answered with some fear.

"Your husband is in the settlement and will come here tonight," Isaac said.

"Tonight!" Eliza exclaimed with joy.

"Yesterday Peter was down at the other station," Isaac said. "Two men and an old woman were there. One of the men said his name is George. From what he told of his history, I'm certain he's your husband. He's a bright, handsome fellow."

"Is he alright?" Eliza asked.

"Yes. He's among friends, who will bring him here."

Release of tension caused Eliza to almost collapse. She went to bed and slept as she hadn't slept since she had fled. She dreamed of a beautiful country of green shores, pleasant islands, and glittering water. In a house that kind voices told her was home, she saw Harry playing, a free and happy child. She heard George's footsteps and felt him coming nearer. His arms were around her. His tears fell on her face, and . . . she awoke! It was no dream. Daylight had faded. Harry lay sleeping by her side. A candle was burning dimly on the night table. George was sobbing by her pillow.

The next morning everyone sat down to a joyful breakfast of cornbread, pancakes, ham, chicken, and coffee. It was the first time that George ever had sat down on equal terms at the table of white people. At first he felt some constraint and awkwardness, but that soon disappeared amid such warmth and kindness.

Buttering his pancakes, Rachel and Isaac's young son Jeremy said, "Father, what if you're found out again?"

"I'd pay my fine," Isaac said quietly.

"What if they put you in prison?" Jeremy asked.

"Couldn't you and Mother manage the farm?" Isaac said, smiling.

"Mother can do almost anything," Jeremy declared.

"You're exposing yourself to danger on our account," George said anxiously to Isaac.

"No, George," Isaac said. "Tonight at ten Phineas Fletcher will take you to the next station. The pursuers are hard after you. We mustn't delay."

"If that's the case, maybe we shouldn't wait until evening," George said.

"It's safer to travel at night," Isaac said. "Today stay here out of sight."

CHAPTER 15

Tom sat among bales of cotton in a little nook on the steamboat's upper deck. By now Haley had come to trust him enough to remove his shackles. Tom could move freely about the boat. He tried to read his Bible, but his thoughts kept returning to his Kentucky home. He imagined Chloe busily preparing a meal, Mose and Pete playing, and Polly sitting on someone's knee. Some tears fell on the pages of his Bible.

Among the steamboat's passengers was a young, wealthy gentleman from New Orleans named Auguste St. Clare. He was elegant and handsome, with large blue eyes and golden hair. With him were his five-year-old daughter Eva and his forty-three-year-old cousin Ophelia, who was in charge of Eva. Tom often had glimpsed the little girl, who always was dressed in white. She was a graceful, beautiful child with golden hair, deep blue eyes, and a rosy mouth. Whenever she saw Haley's chained slaves, she looked at them with bewilderment and sorrow. Several times she brought them candy, nuts, and oranges.

Tom made toys for Eva. He carved faces onto hickory nuts and carved whistles and figures out of wood. Eva shyly accepted Tom's gifts. Finally Tom asked, "What's your name?"

"Eva St. Clare," she answered. "What's yours?"

"Tom. Back home in Kentucky, children called me Uncle Tom."

"Then, I'll call you Uncle Tom, too. Where are you going?"

"I don't know, Miss Eva. I'm going to be sold to someone, but I don't know who."

"My papa can buy you!" Eva said enthusiastically. "I'll ask him today."

"Thank you," Tom said.

The steamboat stopped at a small landing to take wood aboard. Hearing her father's voice, Eva bounded away. Eva and her father were standing by the railings to see the steamboat resume travel when a lurch of the boat made Eva lose her balance. She fell overboard and sank. Before Auguste realized what had happened, Tom dove in. In a moment Eva rose to the surface. Tom caught her in his arms and, swimming with her to the side of the boat, handed her up to outstretched arms. Auguste bore her, dripping but healthy, to the ladies' cabin to be looked after.

The next day the steamboat approached New Orleans. Tom sat on the upper deck, looking anxiously at Auguste. With a pocketbook lying open before him, Auguste was listening, half amused, half contemptuous, to Haley, who was loudly describing Tom's selling points. "He's broad-chested and strong as a horse," Haley said. "Smart, too. He managed his master's farm. And he's religious: humble and pious. The whole world couldn't tempt him to do anything that he thinks is wrong. Besides, your little girl seems set on him." Haley asked $1,300 for Tom.

"Show me your papers," Auguste said. Haley laid a greasy pocketbook on the cotton bales and glanced at certain papers in it.

"Papa, please buy him!" Eva whispered, climbing onto a package and putting her arms around her father's neck. "I want him."

"What for, Eva? Are you going to use him as a rocking horse?" Auguste joked.

"I want to make him happy," Eva said.

"An original reason!" Auguste said.

Haley handed over a certificate signed by Arthur Shelby. Auguste glanced at it. "You see in this letter what Tom's old master says about him," Haley said.

Auguste took out a roll of bills, handed it to Haley, and said, "Count out your money." Haley beamed. After counting out the money and pocketing it, he filled out a bill of sale and handed it to Auguste. "I wonder how much I'd bring if *I* were divided up and inventoried," Auguste said. "How much for the shape of my head; my high forehead; my hands, arms, and legs. How much for my education, talent, honesty, and religion. Not much for the last," he quipped. Taking his daughter's hand, he said, "Come, Eva." They stepped across the boat to Tom. Auguste said, "How do you like your new master, Tom?"

Tears of joy came to Tom's eyes. "God bless you, Master!"

"Well, I hope he *will*. Can you drive horses, Tom?"

"Yes. I'm good with horses," Tom said.

"Then, you'll be our coachman, provided that you won't be drunk more than once a week," Auguste joked.

Surprised and somewhat offended, Tom said, "I never drink, Master."

Seeing Tom's grave expression, Auguste good-humoredly said, "Never mind, my boy. I don't doubt that you intend to do well."

"I certainly do, Master," Tom said.

"You'll be happy," Eva said. "Papa is good to everyone, except that he makes fun of them."

CHAPTER 16

Auguste was the son of a wealthy Louisiana planter. He had married a tall, dark-eyed beauty, Marie, who also was the child of a wealthy plantation owner. Marie was selfish and cold. After giving birth to Eva, she soon had become jealous of Auguste's devotion to the child. Inactive and chronically discontented, Marie was a complainer who constantly imagined herself to be ill. Half the time she lay in bed complaining of a headache. Marie paid little attention to Eva. All household arrangements fell to the St. Clares' slaves.

Auguste was anxious to have someone to look after Eva, so he and Eva had visited his uncle's Vermont farm, where Auguste had persuaded Ophelia to come live with them in New Orleans. Tall and angular, Ophelia had a thin and rather sharp face, compressed lips, and keen, dark eyes. All her movements were decided and energetic. Whenever she spoke, her words were direct and to the point. Ophelia always did what she regarded as her duty. She loved Auguste like a son. When he had been a boy, she had taught him his religious lessons, mended his clothes, and combed his hair. Ophelia adored Eva as well.

Wearing a brown linen traveling dress, Ophelia now sat in her stateroom, surrounded by carpet bags, boxes, and baskets that she was packing and tying up. "We're ready," she said to Eva when she finished. "Where's your papa?"

"He's in the gentlemen's cabin," Eva said.

"Please run and tell him that we're almost there."

Ophelia had a porter bring the baggage out onto the deck. With heavy groans, the steamboat began to push up among the others at the New Orleans landing. Auguste came sauntering up. "A carriage is waiting," he said to Ophelia. Turning to the driver, he said, "Take these things."

"Where's Tom?" Eva asked.

"He's waiting at the carriage," her father answered.

Upon arriving at the St. Clare residence, the carriage passed through an arched gateway into a square courtyard surrounded by an old mansion. Wide galleries with round arches and slender pillars ran along the four sides. In the middle of the courtyard, a fountain tossed water into a marble basin bordered with fragrant violets. The fountain's clear water was alive with gold and silver fishes who darted through it like jewels. A mosaic walk encircled the fountain. This walk was surrounded by smooth grass ornamented with marble vases holding tropical flowers. Two large orange-trees, fragrant with blossoms, stood on the grass.

Eva eagerly said, "Isn't it beautiful, Aunt Ophelia?"

"It's a pretty place," Ophelia replied, "although it doesn't look very Christian."

Tom got down from the carriage and looked around with delight. "Tom, my boy, this seems to suit you," Auguste said.

"Yes, Master," Tom said.

Trunks were hustled off the carriage. A crowd of slaves came running through the galleries, above and below, to greet Auguste and Eva. Foremost among them was a young mulatto man, Louis, dressed in fine clothes, including white pants and a satin vest with gold buttons. "Get back. I'm ashamed of you," Louis said to the other slaves in a tone of authority. "Let Master have some peace."

Auguste paid the driver and turned to Louis, who gracefully bowed. "How are you, Louis?" Auguste said. "See to the baggage. I'll come to all of you in a minute."

Auguste led Ophelia to a large parlor that opened onto the veranda. Eva flew through the parlor to her mother's bedroom. Marie half rose from the couch on which she was reclining.

"Mamma!" Eva cried, throwing her arms around her mother and hugging her tightly.

Marie languidly kissed Eva and said, "That's enough now. Don't make my head ache."

Auguste came in, embraced his wife, and introduced her to Ophelia. Marie observed Ophelia with curiosity and received her with cool politeness.

A group of slaves pressed into the doorway. Among them was a respectable-looking, middle-aged mulatto woman named Belle, who stood in a tremor of expectation. "Mammy!" Eva cried. She ran across the room, threw herself into Belle's arms, and kissed her repeatedly. Laughing and crying with joy, Belle hugged Eva.

Ophelia was taken aback. "Auguste, I believe in being kind to Negroes," she said, "but I can't imagine kissing one."

With a laugh Auguste went out into the passage and distributed pieces of change among his slaves. There was an abundance of laughing and blessing. "Now take yourselves off like good boys and girls," he said to the whole gathering, which disappeared through a door onto a large veranda. Eva followed the slaves. From a bag she distributed apples, nuts, candy, ribbons, laces, and toys that she had collected throughout her homeward journey.

As Auguste turned to go back into Marie's room, he noticed Tom, who was standing uneasily, shifting from one foot to the other. "I'm sorry, Tom," he said. "Come and meet your mistress." When Tom entered the room, he was awed by the velvet carpets and splendid mirrors, paintings, statues, and curtains. "Marie," Auguste said, "this is your new coachman, Tom. Don't say I never think about you when I'm gone. He's a very solemn fellow."

Without rising, Marie fixed her eyes on Tom. "He'll get drunk."

"No. He doesn't drink," Auguste said.

"Well, perhaps he'll turn out well," Marie said begrudgingly.

"Louis," Auguste said, "show Tom downstairs."

Louis moved forward with quick, light steps. With a sturdy tread, Tom followed.

CHAPTER 17

Ophelia took over supervision of the house and of Eva. Marie warned her, "Eva needs looking after. She likes to be with the slaves. I always played with my father's little Negroes, and it never did me any harm. But Eva treats them like equals. I haven't been able to break her of the habit. I think that Auguste encourages her. I believe in being kind to slaves, but they should know their place. Eva doesn't understand that."

"I don't know anything about it, and I thank God that I don't," Ophelia said shortly.

"Well, you'll *have* to know something about it if you stay here," Marie replied. "Our Negroes are stupid, careless, ungrateful, provoking wretches. Auguste says we're responsible for all their faults. That's nonsense. They belong to a degraded race. I keep the whip on hand, and sometimes I use it, but the exertion always strains me. Auguste should send them to be flogged since he won't do it himself. You'll find they need some severity. They're deceitful and lazy."

Eva's merry laugh rose from the courtyard. Ophelia went to the railing. Tom sat in the courtyard. One of his buttonholes was stuck full of white flowers. Eva hung a wreath of roses around his neck. Then she sat on his knee. "Oh, Tom, you look so funny!" Eva said. In his quiet way Tom seemed to be having as much fun as Eva.

Ophelia fetched Auguste to show him what was taking place. "How can you let her?" she asked him.

"Why not?" Auguste said. "You Northerners are odd. You're indignant at the wrongs inflicted on Negroes, yet you loathe Negroes. You object to their being abused, but you want nothing to do with them. You'd like to send them all back to Africa, wouldn't you?" Leaning on the railing, Auguste watched as Eva skipped off, with Tom following.

Eva was so fond of Tom that she asked her father to let Tom escort her whenever she went on walks or rides. Auguste agreed. Tom's stable duties were light, primarily supervision of a stable hand. When he went out, Tom wore a suit of fine cotton, faultless wristbands, a collar, polished boots, and a silk top hat.

On Sunday morning Marie stood on the veranda in a dress of silk and lace. She clasped a diamond bracelet around her slender wrist. Marie was very religious on Sundays. Ophelia stood at her side in an equally fine silk dress and shawl. "I wish Auguste would go to church," Marie said. "He hasn't a shred of religious feeling. It really isn't respectable."

Later that day at dinner Auguste asked, "Well, ladies, how was the sermon?"

"It expressed all of my own feelings," Marie said. "The minister showed how the order of society comes from God. Some people must be high and others low. Some are born to rule and others to serve. He showed that the Bible approves of slavery. I wish you'd heard him."

"We have slaves because it serves our interests to have them," Auguste said. "That's the long and short of it. It certainly has nothing to do with the Bible. Few people care about doing the right thing. Most care only about doing no more wrong than most of the people around them. When slaveholders tell the truth, they say that slavery benefits them, so they want it to continue. That's all."

"Well," Ophelia said to Auguste, "do you think slavery is right or wrong?"

"I'm not going to answer that. If I do, you'll have all sorts of other questions for me."

"I think slavery is right," Marie said. "I'm glad it exists."

The next morning Tom sat in a small loft over the stable. It was a decent room, with a bed, chair, and small, rough stand. Having asked Eva for a sheet of paper, he was trying to write a letter. Eva alighted, like a bird, on the back of his chair and peeped over his shoulder. Seeing Tom's many errors, she exclaimed, "Uncle Tom, what funny scribbles you're making!"

"I'm trying to write to my poor wife and little children, Miss Eva. I've had very little training in writing, so it's hard for me."

"It's a shame you had to leave your family," Eva said. "I'll ask Papa to let you go back some time."

"My mistress said she'd buy me back as soon as she could. I want to send a letter to let them know where I am and to tell Chloe—that's my wife—that I'm doing well. I'm sure she's terribly worried about me."

Auguste now came into the loft and looked at the sheet of paper. "What's this?" he asked.

"Tom's trying to write a letter to his family," Eva said.

"You'd better let me do it for you, Tom," Auguste said. "I'll do it when I get back from my ride."

"Thank you, Master!" Tom said.

"Now get the horses out, Tom," Auguste said.

That evening Auguste wrote Tom's letter and had it mailed.

CHAPTER 18

As the sun was setting, George and Eliza sat hand in hand in Eliza's small bedroom. Harry was on George's knee. "When we get to Canada, I'll do dressmaking," Eliza said. "I also can do washing and ironing."

"We'll be fine as long as we have each other and Harry," George said. "When we're together, I feel rich and strong, although we have nothing but our bare hands. If they'll only leave us alone, I'll be satisfied."

"We aren't out of danger yet," Eliza said.

Someone knocked, and Eliza opened the door. Isaac was there with Phineas, a tall, lanky, red-haired man with an alert expression. "Phineas has learned something important," Isaac said. "Come into the parlor."

When everyone had gathered in the parlor, Phineas said, "Last night I stopped at a small inn back on the road," Phineas began. "I overheard some men who were drinking and talking. One of them said, 'No doubt, they're up in the Quaker settlement.' Then I listened with all my might. They said that they'd send George back to his master in Kentucky, who would make an example of him. They want to sell Eliza in New Orleans and pocket the money, which they think would be about seventeen hundred dollars. They said that the child would go to a slave trader who had bought him. They plan to give Jim and his mother back to their masters in Kentucky. These men also said that two law officers would go with them to capture the runaways. They said that they'd bring Eliza before a judge and one of them would swear that she's his property, so that she'd be handed over to him and he could take her south. They know about the route we were planning to take tonight. They'll be waiting for us with about eight men. What should we do?"

Isaac looked thoughtful. Eliza threw her arms around George and looked up at him. George stood with clenched hands and flashing eyes. "I know what *I'll* do," he said. "I'll have my pistols ready. They intend to use Eliza as a prostitute. I'll fight to the death rather than let them take Eliza and Harry."

"I pray there won't be any violence," Isaac said.

"I don't want to involve anyone else," George said. "Phineas, if you'll lend us your wagon and direct me, Jim and I will drive to the next station, with Jim's mother, Eliza, and Harry inside the wagon. Jim and I both are strong and not afraid to fight."

"You're quite welcome to do all the fighting," Phineas said, "but I know the road and you don't. Please let me drive."

"I don't want to involve you," George insisted.

"Phineas is a wise man. I think you should take his advice," Isaac said, laying his hand on George's shoulder.

"We'd better go without further delay," George said.

"I came with all speed," Phineas said. "They're two or three hours from here. I still think we should wait until dark. I'll go to Michael Cross and ask him to keep watch on the road. He'll come warn us if any of the men are approaching. Michael has a fast horse. I'll also go warn Jim and his mother and tell them to get ready. We have a good chance of reaching the next station before the slave hunters reach us. Don't lose heart, George. This isn't the first ugly scrape I've been in with runaways." Phineas left.

After dark a large covered wagon drew up to the door. Phineas jumped down from his seat to arrange his passengers. With Harry on one arm and Eliza on the other, George left the house and came up to the wagon. Rachel and Isaac also came out.

"Get out for a moment," Phineas said to

those inside. "Let me fix the back of the wagon for the women and the boy."

"Here are two buffalo hides," Rachel said. "Make the seats comfortable. It's hard to ride all night."

Jim emerged from the wagon, assisting his elderly mother, Betty, who clung to his arm and looked anxiously about as if she expected the slave hunters at any moment. "Jim, are your pistols in order?" George asked.

"Yes," Jim said.

Eliza and Rachel exchanged affectionate goodbyes, and Isaac handed Eliza into the wagon. Eliza crept into the back part with Harry and sat among the buffalo hides. Betty was handed in next and seated. George and Jim sat on a board seat in front of the women. Phineas mounted in front.

"Farewell, my friends," Isaac said.

"God bless you!" everyone inside the wagon said to Isaac and Rachel.

The wagon drove off, rattling and jolting over the frozen road. Harry soon fell asleep in Eliza's lap. Eventually Eliza and Betty also slept. Hour after hour the carriage rumbled through woodland, over plains, up hills, and down valleys.

About five o'clock George heard a horse's hoofs some distance behind them. He jogged Phineas by the elbow. Phineas pulled up the horses and listened. "That must be Michael," he said.

"I think I recognize the sound of his gallop." Phineas rose and looked back anxiously over the road. Phineas, George, and Jim now dimly saw a man riding toward them in great haste. "There he is!" Phineas cried. George and Jim sprang out of the wagon and stood awaiting the messenger. "Michael!" Phineas called.

"Phineas!" Michael replied.

"What news? Are they coming?" Phineas asked.

"They're right behind me—about nine of them, hot with brandy, swearing and foaming." A breeze brought the faint sound of galloping horses.

"In! Quickly!" Phineas cried. George and Jim jumped in. Phineas lashed the horses to a run. The wagon rattled, jumped, almost flew over the frozen ground. But the pursuing horsemen approached. Now wide awake, the women looked out. They saw a party of men on a distant hill, against the dawn's red-streaked sky. The slave hunters had caught sight of the wagon, whose white top made it conspicuous. A brutal yell of triumph came forward on the wind. Eliza pressed Harry to her chest. Betty groaned and prayed. George and Jim clenched their pistols.

The slave hunters quickly gained on the runaways. Phineas raced the wagon toward some rocks. Suddenly checking his horses, he sprang from his seat and cried, "Out, everyone! We're going up into these rocks! Michael, tie your horse to the wagon and drive the wagon to Amariah's, so that the slave hunters can't take away our means of escape. Then return with the wagon and with help."

Everyone hurried out of the wagon. Grabbing Harry, Phineas yelled, "Run!" Everyone raced for the rocks. Throwing himself from his horse, Michael fastened the bridle to the wagon and rapidly drove the wagon away.

As he reached the rocks, Phineas cried, "Come!" A rough footpath ran up among the rocks. With Harry in his arms, Phineas led the way, springing up the rocks like a goat. Jim came second, bearing Betty over his shoulder. George and Eliza brought up the rear.

The horsemen came up to the rocks. Shouting and cursing, they dismounted.

A few moments' scrambling brought the runaways to a chasm more than a yard wide. Beyond it lay a steep pile of rocks. Phineas easily leaped the chasm and sat Harry down on a flat platform. "Jump!" he cried. "Jump for your lives!" One after another sprang across. Several fragments of loose stone formed a kind of barricade that sheltered their position from the observation of those below. Phineas peeped over the barricade to watch the pursuers. "Whoever comes up here has to walk single file between those two rocks, in fair range of your pistols," he said to George and Jim.

The pursuers paused and appeared to debate. They consisted of Loker, Marks, two law officers, and a posse of drunken rowdies who thought it would be fun to catch some "niggers." "Well, Ted, your coons are treed," one said.

"I'm for going right up," Loker said.

"They might fire at us from behind the rocks," Marks said.

"Nah!" Loker scoffed. "They're too scared."

George appeared on a rock above them. "We have weapons," he called down. "The first one of you who comes within range of our bullets is a dead man. We'll kill every one of you."

A short, puffy man stepped forward and said, "We're law officers. Give up peacefully."

"We don't acknowledge your laws," George answered. "We'll fight for our freedom."

A brief silence followed. Marks cocked his pistol. "You said you'd get as much for him dead as alive," he said to Loker, and he fired at George.

George sprang backward. Eliza screamed. The ball passed close to George's head and lodged in a tree. "I'm fine, Eliza," George said quickly.

"Stay out of sight," Phineas said.

"Jim," George said, "Watch the pass with me. I'll fire at the first man who shows himself. You take the second, and so on."

"What if you miss?" Jim asked.

"I won't," George said coolly.

The group below stood undecided. "I think you hit one of them," one of the men said. "I heard a scream."

"I'm going up," Loker said. "I've never been afraid of niggers, and I don't aim to start now. Come on." He sprang up the rocks.

George pointed his pistol at the spot in the pass where the first man would appear. A man followed Loker, and the rest began pushing their way up the rocks. In a moment Loker's burly form appeared almost at the verge of the chasm. George fired. The shot entered Loker's side, but Loker didn't retreat. Instead, with a yell of rage he leaped across the chasm. Stepping to the front, Phineas pushed Loker backward. Loker fell into the chasm thirty feet below, crackling down among trees, bushes, logs, and stones. He lay injured and groaning.

"Pick up Ted while I ride back for help," Marks said, fleeing. He galloped away as the others hooted and jeered.

"Damned coward!" one of the men said.

The men scrambled through stumps, logs, and bushes to Loker, who lay groaning and swearing. "Are you badly hurt?" one asked.

"I don't know," Loker answered. "Get me up." Supporting Loker under each of his shoulders, two men got Loker to the horses. "Get me back to the inn," Loker said. "Give me a handkerchief or something to stop the bleeding."

Phineas looked over the rocks and saw men trying to lift Loker into the saddle. After two futile attempts, Loker fell heavily to the ground. "They're leaving him!" Phineas said in surprise. All of Loker's companions got onto their horses and rode away. When they were out of sight, Phineas said, "I told Michael to go on ahead, fetch help, and come back with the wagon. We'll have to walk some distance along the road to meet them. God grant that Michael comes soon! We aren't much more than two miles from the next station."

As the group neared the foot of the rocks, they saw the wagon returning, accompanied by some men on horseback. "It's Michael, Joseph, and Amariah! We're safe!" Phineas cried.

"Shouldn't we do something for him?" Eliza asked, referring to Loker.

Phineas kneeled by Loker and examined his condition. Using his pocket handkerchief, Phineas prepared a bandage to stanch the bleeding. "You pushed me," Loker said faintly to Phineas.

"If I hadn't, you would've pushed *us*," Phineas responded. "We'll take you to a house where you'll be cared for." Loker groaned and shut his eyes.

Michael, Joseph, and Amariah arrived. The seats were removed from the wagon, the buffalo hides were spread along one side, and four men, with great difficulty, lifted Loker onto the hides. Before he was in, he fainted. The runaways got into the wagon, and it moved forward. "Do you think he'll die?" George asked Phineas.

"No. It's only a flesh wound."

"I'm glad," George said. "I wouldn't want to be responsible for his death."

A ride of about an hour brought the group to a neat farmhouse, where the weary travelers were given an abundant breakfast. Loker was deposited in a clean, soft bed. Dorcas Pryor carefully dressed and bandaged his wound. She was a tall, dignified Quaker with thoughtful gray eyes and silver hair parted on a broad, clear forehead. Her brown silk dress rustled as she glided up and down the room.

Loker regained consciousness. "I suppose the runaways are here," he said. Dorcas didn't say anything. "They'd better be off to Lake Erie. The quicker the better," Loker said. Dorcas sat and started to knit. "We have people in Sandusky who watch the boats for us," Loker continued. Dorcas now listened intently. "Tell that to the runaways," Loker said. "I hope they get away, just to spite Marks. Damn the bastard."

"Please don't use such language!" Dorcas objected.

"Tell them to disguise the quadroon woman. Her description is out in Sandusky."

Because of Loker's warnings, Jim and Betty left that night. The next night, George, Eliza, and Harry were driven into Sandusky. Ruth Smyth, a middle-aged woman from a Quaker settlement in Canada, was with them, pretending to be Harry's aunt. Eliza's hair had been cut short, and she was dressed like a man. Harry was dressed like a girl.

"We're only twenty-four hours from Canada," George said to Eliza. "One day and night on Lake Erie, and we'll be there. Are we really about to be free?"

"I'm sure of it," Eliza said.

A cab drove the four to the wharf, where they boarded the steamboat. Ruth took Harry to the ladies' cabin. George went to purchase tickets at the ship's office, where he overheard an exchange between the ship's clerk and Marks.

"I've watched everyone who came on board," the clerk said. "They aren't on this boat."

"The woman could be mistaken for a white," Marks said. "The man is a very light mulatto with a brand on one hand."

As George took the tickets, his hands trembled a bit, but he turned around coolly, glanced at Marks, and strolled to another part of the boat, where Eliza stood waiting for him. As the ship's bell gave a farewell peal, Marks walked down the plank to the shore.

George sighed with relief as the steamboat headed out onto Lake Erie. The lake sparkled in the sun. A fresh breeze blew. George and Eliza walked up and down the deck. The boat swept on.

At last, Canada's shores came into view. George and Eliza stood arm in arm as the boat neared the town of Amherstberg. Tears came to their eyes. They squeezed each other's hand. The bell rang, and the boat stopped. George gathered their baggage, and he, Eliza, Harry, and Ruth disembarked.

As soon as they were out of the view of strangers, George and Eliza embraced and wept. Ruth guided the family to the home of a good missionary. Eliza and George were unable to sleep that night. They felt too much joy.

CHAPTER 19

One day when Ophelia, Tom, and Dinah the cook were in the kitchen, a tall, bony old black woman entered, bearing on her head a basket of muffins and hot rolls.

"Prue, you've come," Dinah said. "Let's see your muffins. Miss Ophelia here will pay for them." Ophelia selected two dozen and paid Prue. "See that you don't spend it on whiskey," Dinah said to Prue.

"You steal your master's money to buy liquor?" Ophelia asked Prue.

"I can't live otherwise. I drink to forget my misery," Prue answered.

"You're wicked and foolish," Ophelia said. "Who's your master?"

"Mr. Landis. He whips me severely every time I drink. I'd stop if I could," Prue said. She rose slowly and stiffly, put her basket on her head, and left.

Dinah said to Ophelia, "Her back's so cut up, it hurts her to slip clothes over it."

Tom followed Prue out into the street. "I'll carry your basket for a while," he said.

"I don't want any help," Prue said coldly, although she strained under her basket's weight.

"I wish I could persuade you to stop drinking," Tom said earnestly. Prue didn't say anything. "Where were you raised?" Tom asked.

"Kentucky. A man kept me to breed children for market and sold them as soon as they were big enough. Finally he sold me to a trader, and Landis bought me."

"What made you start drinking?"

Prue stopped, set her basket down, adjusted the old, faded shawl that covered her shoulders, and said, "It was the only thing that eased my pain. I had one child, Jeannie, after I came here. She was the prettiest thing! At first Jeannie never cried. She was strong and plump. But Mrs. Landis took sick, and I had to tend her. I caught the fever, and my milk stopped. Jeannie shriveled to skin and bones. Mrs. Landis wouldn't let her have any milk. Jeannie cried day and night. Mrs. Landis took her away from me each night, saying that Jeannie's crying kept me awake so that I wasn't fit for work. Mrs. Landis made me sleep in her room while Jeannie was put in an attic, where she cried and cried. One night Jeannie died. She had starved. I started drinking to drown out the memory of her crying." With a groan, Prue put her basket back atop her head and walked away.

Tom walked sorrowfully back to the house.

A few days later a woman other than Prue brought the muffins and rolls. "Where's Prue?" Dinah asked.

"She won't be coming anymore," the woman said.

"Why not?" Dinah asked.

Glancing at Ophelia, the woman gave no reply. After she had selected muffins, Ophelia said, "Tell me what's happened."

Reluctantly the woman said, "Prue got drunk again, and Mr. Landis had her down in the cellar all day. She's dead. They must have whipped her to death." Tom now shared what Prue had told him about her history, especially her baby.

"What an abominable business! It's horrific!" Ophelia exclaimed. She hurried to the room where Auguste was reading the newspaper. "Prue has been whipped to death!" Ophelia said with horror.

"I thought it would come to that," Auguste said calmly.

"You thought...? And you did nothing? Will you do something *now*?"

"If people choose to ruin their own possessions, that's their business," Auguste said. "Prue was a thief and a drunkard. No one will have much sympathy for her."

"This is outrageous, Auguste!" Ophelia exclaimed.

"If low-minded, brutal owners such as Landis will act as they do, what can *I* do about it?"

"You can report them to the authorities!"

"With regard to such a case, there's no law that amounts to anything. Let it go, Ophelia."

"Let it go? This is unbelievable."

"No, it's exactly what you can expect when one set of people has absolute control over another. You've just begun to glimpse what goes on." Auguste returned to his newspaper.

Stunned, Ophelia sat down. After a time she said, "I can't just push things out of my mind as you do. How can you possibly think that slavery is right?"

"I never said that I think that slavery is right," Auguste replied. "Surely you know that people are always doing things that they know are wrong."

"Are you saying that day after day you continue to do what you know to be wrong?" Ophelia said.

"Of course I think it's wrong," Auguste said. "Slavery is nothing more than the politically and economically powerful taking advantage of the weak. People hold slaves because they *can*. If something is hard, dirty, or otherwise disagreeable, why not make someone else do it? If you can get free labor, why pay for labor? That's the attitude. The slave does the work; the owner profits from it. That's what slavery is all about.

No matter how coarse, ignorant, and cruel a white is, they can own a slave and treat that slave as they wish. As has happened with Prue, a slave's owner can whip them to death. I think that many slaveholders feel as I do about slavery. They even realize that slavery is bad for the master and mistress as well as for the slave. Slavery encourages vice in the owners: laziness, dependence, and cruelty. In the end I'm simply too weak and selfish to free my slaves."

At tea Marie commented on Prue's death. "Some of these creatures are so bad that they don't deserve to live. I don't feel a particle of sympathy for such cases. If they'd behave themselves, it wouldn't happen."

"But, Mamma," Eva protested, "Prue suffered from cruelty. That's what made her drink."

"Rubbish! I've probably suffered more than she *ever* did," Marie said. "You don't see *me* stealing or getting drunk."

CHAPTER 20

Finding Tom to be both trustworthy and sensible with money, Auguste increasingly entrusted his business to Tom. Auguste would hand bills to Tom without looking at them and pocket the change that Tom gave him without counting it. Tom regarded his frivolous master with a mixture of loyalty and fatherly concern. Because Auguste never read the Bible or went to church, and mocked everyone and everything, Tom feared for Auguste's soul and prayed for him.

One morning while Ophelia was sewing, Auguste called to her from the parlor. "Cousin, I have something to show you." When Ophelia entered the parlor, Auguste said, "I've made a purchase. Here." He presented a black girl about eight years old. She was very dark. Her round, shining eyes glanced around the room. Her kinky hair was arranged in small braids that stuck out in every direction. She wore a filthy, ragged dress made of bagging and stood with her hands folded in front of her.

With dismay Ophelia said, "Auguste, what in the world have you brought that thing here for?"

"For you to educate and train. I found her amusing in a minstrel-show sort of way." Giving a whistle, as someone might to attract a dog's attention, Auguste said, "Topsy, give us a song and dance." Topsy sang in a shrill voice while spinning, clapping her hands, and knocking her knees together in time to the music. She ended with a somersault. Ophelia stood silent with amazement. Enjoying Ophelia's reaction, Auguste said, "Topsy, this is your new mistress. See that you behave."

"Yes, Master," Topsy said.

"Auguste, your house already is full of these little plagues," Ophelia protested. "It's impossible to walk without stepping on one of them. I get up in the morning and find one asleep behind the door, see another lying on the doormat, and see faces grinning between all the railings. Why on earth did you buy another?"

"I told you—so that you can educate her. You're always preaching about educating, so I'm making you a present of a fresh-caught specimen."

"I don't want her. I already have more to do with Negroes than I want to."

"She belonged to a couple of drunkards who keep a low-class restaurant that I have to pass every day. I was tired of hearing them swear at her and tired of hearing her scream as they beat her. Plus, she looked bright and funny. So I bought her. Think of her as a sort of missionary project. See if you can turn her into a good Christian."

"Well, I'll do what I can," Ophelia said. "She's dreadfully dirty."

"Take her downstairs. Have someone clean and dress her," Auguste said.

Ophelia carried Topsy down to the kitchen. "I don't see what Master wants with another nigger," Dinah said, observing the new arrival with disgust. "I don't want her under my feet."

"The low little nigger should keep out of my way," the maid Rosa said.

With Rosa's reluctant assistance, Ophelia washed and dressed Topsy. She saw large welts and calluses on Topsy's back and shoulders. Pointing to the marks, Rosa said, "Look at that! That shows that she's trouble."

Topsy soon was dressed in decent clothes, with her hair cut close to her head. Sitting in front of her, Ophelia asked, "How old are you, Topsy?"

"I don't know, Mistress," Topsy answered.

"Who were your parents?" Ophelia asked.

"I don't know. A trader raised me with lots of others."

"What did you do for your master and mistress? Did you sew?" Ophelia asked.

"I never sewed, but I can fetch water, wash dishes, sharpen knives, and wait on folks," Topsy said.

The next day in her bedroom, Ophelia instructed Topsy in making a bed with the sheets tucked in smoothly and tightly. After each instruction Topsy said, "Yes, ma'am." At one point, while Ophelia's back was turned, Topsy snatched a pair of gloves and a ribbon and slipped them into her sleeves.

"Now, Topsy, let's see you do it," Ophelia said after she had finished her demonstration. To Ophelia's amazement Topsy performed the task flawlessly. As she finished, however, the tip of the stolen ribbon protruded from one of her sleeves. Noticing it, Ophelia cried, "What's this? You stole it!" Ophelia pulled the ribbon out.

"That's Miss Ophelia's ribbon?" Topsy said with feigned innocence. "It must have gotten caught in my sleeve."

"So, you lie as well as steal!"

"I never tell lies," Topsy lied.

"If you tell lies, I'll have to whip you."

Topsy began to cry but persisted in lying. "Miss Ophelia must have left the ribbon where it got caught in my sleeve."

Ophelia was so indignant at the barefaced lie that she grabbed Topsy and shook her. "Stop lying!" The glove now fell from Topsy's other sleeve. "You little thief! Confess to taking the

gloves and the ribbon, and I won't whip you."
Topsy confessed. "I let you run about all day yesterday, so you must have taken other things in
the house," Ophelia said. "Tell me, and I won't
whip you. What else did you take?"

"I took Miss Eva's red necklace."

"Naughty child! What else did you take?"

"I took Rosa's red earrings."

Eva and Rosa now entered. Eva was wearing
her red necklace, and Rosa was wearing her red
earrings. Ophelia was bewildered. "Why did you
tell me you took the necklace and earrings,
Topsy?"

"You said I had to confess," Topsy said, "and
I didn't have anything else to confess to."

"I didn't want you to confess to things you
didn't do," Ophelia said with exasperation.
"That's telling a lie just as much as denying
things you *did* do."

"So, she's a little liar as well as a dirty low-
down thing!" Rosa said. "Mistress should whip
her 'til she bleeds."

"Don't talk like that, Rosa," Eva said.
Cowed, Rosa left the room. Eva gently said,
"You don't need to steal here, Topsy. You'll be
well taken care of. If you really want something
that belongs to me, just ask me for it and I'll give
it to you." Having never known genuine kindness, let alone generosity, Topsy didn't believe
Eva.

To punish Topsy, Ophelia locked her in a closet for several hours. "I don't see how I'm going to manage that child without whipping her," Ophelia told Auguste.

"Whip her, then," he said. "Do whatever you like. But I'll say this: I've seen that child be hit with pokers and shovels, so your whippings won't make much of an impression on her unless they're very energetic. Are you prepared to brutalize both yourself and the child?" Ophelia was not.

All the other children, including Eva, found Topsy's singing, dancing, and acrobatics immensely entertaining. Noticing that Eva liked to be with Topsy, Ophelia asked Auguste to forbid the association. "Topsy will teach her mischief," Ophelia said.

"No one can teach Eva mischief," Auguste said confidently.

Whenever another slave insulted Topsy, they soon paid for the insult. They would find some cherished trinket missing or some article of clothing ruined. Or they would stumble into a pail of hot water or be covered with slop poured onto them from above. Although everyone thought Topsy responsible for these occurrences, no one ever could prove her guilt. Soon everyone thought it wisest to leave Topsy in peace.

Ophelia instituted regular hours and activities for Topsy and taught her to read and sew. Topsy enjoying reading but found sewing boring.

On Sundays Ophelia taught Topsy the catechism. Topsy quickly learned all the skills that Ophelia taught her. No one was better than Topsy at smoothing sheets, adjusting pillows, or dusting and arranging objects. But she would *do* these things only when watched. Unwatched, she would pull off pillowcases, toss sheets, and put on Ophelia's clothes.

Once, Topsy wrapped Ophelia's best shawl around her head as a turban, and Ophelia caught Topsy admiring herself in the mirror. Ophelia whipped Topsy, who groaned and screamed. Half an hour later Topsy told a group of admiring children, "Miss Ophelia's whippings are nothing. They wouldn't kill a mosquito. My old master knew how to whip. He'd make my flesh fly off."

One day Ophelia entered her bedroom and gave a loud exclamation. She soon appeared before Auguste, dragging Topsy. "What has Topsy done now?" Auguste asked.

"She cut bonnet trimming to pieces to make dolls' jackets! I don't know what to do. I've tried everything I can think of with this child. She *won't* behave."

"Topsy," Auguste said, "why do you misbehave? Miss Ophelia says she has tried everything with you."

"My old mistress used to say the same thing. She'd whip me, pull my hair, and knock my head against the door."

Eva, who had been listening, motioned to Topsy, who followed Eva into a sunroom at the corner of the veranda. "Why won't you try to be good, Topsy?" Eva asked earnestly. "Don't you love anyone?"

"I love candy and such," Topsy said. "Otherwise I don't know anything about love. I never had any family."

"But if you were good, you..."

"If I were good, I'd still be a nigger," Topsy said.

"People can love you if you're a Negro. Miss Ophelia would love you if you were good," Eva said.

Topsy gave a short laugh of disbelief. "She can't bear me because I'm a nigger. Whites can't love niggers."

"God loves you as much as he loves any white," Eva said. "*I* love you, and it grieves me that you're naughty. Please be good for my sake."

"I'll try," Topsy said.

CHAPTER 21

Sitting in one chair and with his heels on another, Arthur Shelby was enjoying his after-dinner cigar. Margaret sat nearby sewing. "Chloe has had a letter from Tom," she said.

"Really? How is he?" Arthur asked.

"Apparently, he was bought by a fine family who treat him kindly and don't make him do much work."

"I'm very glad," Arthur said heartily. "He might not want to return here."

"To the contrary," Margaret said, "he asks very anxiously when we'll be able to buy him back."

"I don't know," Arthur said. "I'm still continually running into debt."

"We could sell some of our paintings, jewelry, and other valuables that don't serve any practical purpose."

"That's ridiculous. You don't understand business matters, Margaret."

"Give me a list of your debts. Let me see if I can help you to economize."

"Leave it alone," Arthur said with annoyance.

"We should find some way to raise the necessary money," Margaret insisted. "Aunt Chloe's heart is set on it."

"You shouldn't have promised anything. It would be best for Chloe to accept that Tom probably won't be back. He'll probably have another wife soon. Chloe should find someone else."

"I've taught our people that marriage is sacred!" Margaret said angrily. "I never would give Chloe such advice. If you won't provide the money, I'll earn it myself. I'll take music pupils."

"I won't consent to that," Arthur said, and he strode from the room.

Chloe now appeared. Not concealing that she had heard every word of the Shelbys' conversation, she said, "If you please, Mistress, you could make money by hiring me out. Sam said that a baker in Louisville is looking for someone to make cakes and pastries. He'll pay four dollars a week to the owners. If you'll let me go, I'll bring in the money."

"But, Chloe," Margaret said, "you'd be leaving your children."

"Mose and Pete are big enough to do a day's work now, and Sally would take care of Polly," Chloe said.

"Louisville is quite a distance away," Margaret said.

"That's alright. I'd be closer to Tom," Chloe said.

"He'd still be hundreds of miles away, Chloe. And you'd have to work four or five years before you'd have enough." Chloe's countenance fell. "Still, I'll let you go if you really want to," Margaret said. "Every cent of your wages will be laid aside to buy Tom." Chloe's face brightened. "When did you want to go?" Margaret asked.

"Tomorrow," Chloe answered.

"Tomorrow! Very well."

"Mistress, would you please have someone write to Tom to tell him about this?" Chloe asked.

"I will, Aunt Chloe."

James Shelby answered Tom's letter. He told Tom that Chloe had been hired out to a Louisville baker to earn money for Tom's return, Mose and Pete were thriving, Polly was trotting all about the house under Sally's care, and all members of the Shelby family were fine.

CHAPTER 22

To escape the heat of New Orleans, the St. Clare family was at its summer cottage on Lake Pontchartrain. Verandas surrounded the cottage. The living room opened onto a large garden, fragrant with tropical plants. The garden's paths ran down to the lake.

As the sun was setting, Tom and Eva sat in an arbor at the foot of the garden. Over the past six months, Eva's hands had become thinner, her skin more transparent, and her breath shorter. Whenever she romped in the garden, she soon tired. She often coughed and burned with fever. Doctors had diagnosed Eva as fatally ill with tuberculosis. "Eva! Eva!" Ophelia called. "You mustn't be outside as it gets colder." Eva and Tom hurried in.

Grief-stricken, Auguste spent much more time with Eva than before. She had become so ill that she was confined to the house. Absorbed in her own imaginary ailments, Marie continued to pay little attention to Eva.

Eva grieved for those she would leave behind, especially her father. One day she said to him, "Papa, I'm going to leave you. I don't mind for myself because I'm going to heaven, but I worry about you and my friends." Auguste gave a single dry sob and pressed Eva to him. "I want our slaves to be free, Papa," Eva said. "If anything happened to you, what would become of them?"

"It's you I worry about," Auguste said.

"That's the problem, Papa. You worry about only me while many people have nothing but pain and sorrow. Will you free our slaves, Papa? Will you do it for my sake? Please promise me that you'll at least free Tom."

"I promise to free Tom," Auguste said. Then he sat silently holding Eva to his chest. As it grew darker, he took her to her bedroom. When she was dressed for bed, he sent the attendants away and rocked her in his arms, softly singing to her until she was asleep.

Increasingly Eva was confined to her bedroom, where she would lie on a small couch by the open window that overlooked the lake. One afternoon she heard her mother on the veranda: "What now, you baggage? You've been picking flowers!" Eva heard a sharp slap.

"They're for Miss Eva!" Topsy cried.

"A pretty excuse!" Marie said. "Do you think she wants flowers from you, a good-for-nothing nigger? Get along!"

In a moment Eva was off her couch and on the veranda. "I *do* want them," she said. Topsy offered Eva the flowers. "What a beautiful bouquet!" Eva said. "You've selected and arranged the flowers so perfectly, Topsy. Thank you." Topsy looked pleased. She made a short curtsy and left.

"Mamma, Topsy is trying to be good," Eva protested. "You should help her along instead of abusing her."

"Abusing her! She constantly abuses *us*. And she's so ugly I hardly can bare to look at her," Marie said.

One day Eva asked her father to have all of the slaves gather in her bedroom. She lay back on her pillows, her hair lying loose about her face, her crimson cheeks contrasting with her skin's sickly whiteness. Because she had become so thin, her eyes looked larger than ever.

When the slaves entered, no one spoke. Eva raised herself and looked long and earnestly at everyone. All looked sad and worried. "I sent for you, my dear friends, because I have something to say to you. Within a few weeks I'll be dead, but I expect to see you all in heaven." There were groans, sobs, and lamentations. Some fell to their knees and prayed.

After each slave had tearfully said goodbye to Eva, all visitors left except Auguste. "Papa," Eva said, gently laying her hand on his. He sobbed.

Ophelia cared for Eva day and night. Tom often visited Eva. He would carry her up and down the room, out onto the veranda, and sometimes around the garden. He also started sleeping on the veranda outside Eva's bedroom, so that he'd be able to rush in and be with her at her last moments. One midnight Ophelia cried out, "Tom, fetch the doctor! There isn't a moment to lose!" Hurrying across the room, Ophelia knocked on Auguste's door. He was up and in Eva's room in an instant. Eva was asleep. Ophelia and Auguste stood there, gazing at her deathly pallor.

Tom soon returned with the doctor. "When did this change take place?" the doctor asked Ophelia.

"About midnight," Ophelia said.

Awakened by the doctor's entrance, Marie rushed in. "Auguste!"

"Hush," Auguste said hoarsely. "She's dying." Stooping over his daughter, he said, "Eva, darling!"

Eva opened her eyes and smiled. "Dear Papa," she said weakly. She struggled for breath.

"Oh, God," Auguste said in agony.

Weeping, Tom said, "It's over, Master. She's gone."

CHAPTER 23

After Eva's funeral the household returned to New Orleans. Softened by Eva's death and the slaves' genuine grief, Ophelia became gentler. She spent more time with Topsy, no longer shrinking from her touch or showing disgust, because she no longer felt any.

Auguste attached himself to Tom more each day, taking comfort in Tom's strength and sympathy. One day Auguste said, "Tom, I'm going to free you. I'm in the legal process of doing that."

Overjoyed, Tom raised his hands to heaven and cried, "Thank the Lord!"

Somewhat annoyed, Auguste asked, "Have you been unhappy here?"

"It's the joy of being free," Tom said.

"I've given you the best of everything and required very little work from you," Auguste said, still somewhat insulted.

"You've been very good to me, Master, but I'd rather have poor clothes, a poor house, poor everything and have them be mine than have the best of what belongs to someone else."

"I suppose so," Auguste said.

"Also, I miss my family so much," Tom said.

"I understand," Auguste said.

That evening Tom sat on the veranda, thinking of home and his coming freedom. He would work to buy Chloe and his children. Suddenly there were loud knocks and many voices at the gate. Startled, Tom hurried to unfasten the gate. Several men carried in Auguste, lying on a shutter and wrapped in a cloak. Tom gave a cry of amazement and despair. It rang through the house, causing all residents to come running.

Auguste had gone to a cafe to read the evening newspaper. As he was reading, a fight had broken out between two drunk men. Auguste and another man had tried to separate the fighters. Auguste had been stabbed in the side with a hunting knife that he had tried to wrest from one of the men.

The house was full of screams and wails. Marie was hysterical. At Ophelia's direction, one of the couches in the parlor was hastily prepared and Auguste, bleeding, was laid on it. He had fainted from pain and blood loss. Ophelia applied restoratives. Auguste opened his eyes.

A doctor arrived. He dressed the wound but declared it fatal. Ophelia ushered the frantic slaves away Only Tom was allowed to stay.

Laying his hand on Tom's, Auguste said, "Tom, I'm dying. Pray for me." Tom wept and prayed. Auguste died with a peaceful expression.

CHAPTER 24

Upon Auguste's death every slave in the St. Clare household felt fear as well as grief. They all knew Marie's unfeeling, tyrannical character.

Two days after Auguste's funeral, Rosa fell to her knees in front of Ophelia and begged, "Oh, Miss Ophelia, please go to Mistress and plead for me! She's going to send me out to be whipped. I'm to get fifteen lashes!"

"What has happened?" Ophelia asked.

"I was trying on Mistress's dress. She slapped my face and, without thinking, I talked back to her."

Ophelia said, "Sit down, child. I'm going to your mistress."

"Oh, thank you, Miss Ophelia. Thank you!"

Ophelia found Marie in her easy chair, with Belle standing and combing Marie's hair. "I want to speak to you about Rosa," Ophelia said, trying to sound civil.

"What about her?" Marie responded sharply.

"She is very sorry about having been insolent," Ophelia said.

"She is, is she? She'll be a lot sorrier before I'm done with her. I've endured her impudence long enough. Now I'll bring her down," Marie said.

"Couldn't you punish her in a less brutal way?" Ophelia said.

"She needs a lesson that she won't forget," Marie said. "She'll lose her uppity airs fast enough."

Unable to restrain her anger, Ophelia said, "You'll answer to God for your cruelty!"

"Cruelty? She'll get only fifteen lashes," Marie said casually.

"Lashes applied by some brutal man who chooses to do that for a living!" Realizing that Marie would remain unmoved, Ophelia left the room. Rosa was taken to the whipping house, where she received the fifteen lashes.

A few days later Tom was standing by the balconies when Louis joined him. Since Auguste's death, Louis had been disconsolate. "Mistress has decided to sell the place and all of us except Belle," Louis said to Tom. "She's going to return to her father's plantation."

"How do you know?" Tom asked.

"I hid behind the curtains when she was talking with her lawyer. We're going to be auctioned off."

Tom's eyes filled with bitter tears. Reunion with his family now seemed impossible. He went to Ophelia. "Miss Ophelia," he said, "Master promised me my freedom. He said he'd begun the legal process. Would you please tell Mistress that Master wanted me to be free?"

"I'll certainly speak for you, Tom, but I don't have much hope," Ophelia said.

Ophelia found Marie reclining on a couch. "I've been wanting to talk to you, Ophelia," Marie said. "I'm going home to my father's plantation, so I'm putting the furniture and most of the slaves up at auction. I'm keeping Belle, and Topsy belongs to *you*."

"Topsy belongs to me?" Ophelia said, bewildered.

"Yes. Auguste bought her for you. The bill of sale names you as her owner."

"I don't want to *own* anyone!" Ophelia declared.

"Then, sell her, or give her to me," Marie said.

Horrified by either of those possibilities, Ophelia said, "No, I'll take care of her." After a pause Ophelia said, "Auguste promised Tom his liberty and began filling out the necessary legal forms. I hope you'll carry through. It was Auguste's wish."

"I'll do no such thing!" Marie said sharply. "Tom is one of the most valuable slaves on the place."

"Auguste promised him," Ophelia said.

"Well, I *didn't*."

Ophelia wrote to Margaret Shelby, explaining Tom's danger, urging her to follow up, and giving Margaret contact information for the St. Clares' lawyer. With this lawyer's assistance, Ophelia freed Topsy. When Ophelia told Topsy that she was free, Topsy had trouble believing it. "Would you like to stay with me, Topsy—until you're a grown-up lady?" Ophelia asked.

Now fond of Ophelia, and frightened at the thought of being among strangers, Topsy emphatically answered, "Yes, Miss Ophelia." Two days later Ophelia and Topsy left for Ophelia's family home in Vermont.

CHAPTER 25

A week later Tom and most of the other St. Clare slaves were marched, at night, to a slave warehouse, where people were sold, leased, mortgaged, and exchanged for items such as groceries. Tom had a sizable trunk of clothing. He was ushered into the sleeping room for men. A large group already was assembled. Tom set his trunk in a corner, sat down on it, and leaned his face against the wall.

A burly black man named Joe came over to Tom, poked him in the side, and asked, "Why are you being sold?"

Tom quietly answered, "My master died."

"What about you?" Joe asked Louis, laying his hand on Louis's shoulder.

"Leave me alone!" Louis said fiercely, straightening with disgust.

"Boys, here's one of those white niggers," Joe mocked. He sniffed Louis. "All cream-colored and scented. He'd do for a tobacco shop. They could keep him to smell snuff."

"I said to leave me alone," Louis fumed.

Imitating Louis's haughty manner, Joe said, "How touchy we white niggers are with our airs and graces. We've been in a good family, haven't we?"

"Yes, I *was* in a good family. I belonged to the St. Clares," Louis said proudly.

"Did you? Well, they must have been glad to get rid of you. I guess they're going to trade you off with a lot of cracked teapots and the like." Joe grinned tauntingly. Enraged, Louis flew at Joe, swearing and striking at him on every side. The gathering laughed and shouted.

The uproar brought slave dealer Roger Skeggs to the door. "Order!" he shouted, coming in and flourishing a large whip. "Go to sleep, all of you!"

In another room about fifty female slaves of all ages slept on the floor, wrapped in blankets or clothing. One ten-year-old girl, whose mother had been sold the day before, cried herself to sleep. A well-dressed mulatto woman named Susan sat in a corner. Around forty-five years old, she had soft eyes and a gentle face. Her fifteen-year-old quadroon daughter Nancy nestled against her. Nancy had curly brown hair and, like her mother, was dressed with great neatness. Her hands were white and delicate. Susan and Nancy had been the personal attendants of an amiable, pious New Orleans lady who had taught them to read and write and had instructed them in religion. When this woman had fallen into debt, she had sold most of her slaves.

"Mother, lay your head on my lap and try to sleep," Nancy said.

"I can't, Nancy. This may be our last night together."

"I pray not!"

With a deadly sickness at her heart, Susan remembered how Skeggs had looked at Nancy's hands, lifted up her curly hair, and pronounced her a "first-rate article." "Tomorrow I want you to pull your hair back straight so it doesn't look so pretty," Susan said. "That will make you more appealing to respectable families and less appealing to... disreputable people."

"I will, Mother."

"If we never see each other again, always remember how you were brought up and . . . that I love you." Susan held Nancy in her arms and wished that Nancy were less beautiful.

In the morning everyone was marched to the auction site. Wearing a straw hat and smoking a cigar, Skeggs walked around to put finishing touches on his wares. Stepping in front of Nancy, he said, "Where are your curls, girl?"

Nancy looked timidly at her mother, who quickly said, "I told her to make her hair smooth and neat so that she'd look respectable."

"Those curls add a hundred dollars to your

price. Loosen your hair!" Skeggs ordered Nancy, who obeyed.

"Hello, Duchenne," a young dandy said, slapping the shoulder of another dandy, who was examining Louis through an eyeglass.

"I want a valet," Duchenne said, "and I heard that St. Clare's lot was going."

"You wouldn't catch me buying any of St. Clare's people. Spoiled niggers—every one of them. Impudent as the devil."

"If I get them, they'll soon lose their airs," Duchenne said. "They'll find they're dealing with a very different kind of master. I like the shape of that fellow," he said of Louis. "I'll buy him."

"It'll take everything you have to keep him. He's extravagant."

"He'll find he can't be extravagant with *me*," Duchenne said. "Just let him be sent to the whipping house a few times. He'll change his ways."

About two hundred men had gathered as potential buyers. Tom anxiously examined one face after another. All of them conveyed callousness.

Simon Legree, a short, broad, muscular man in worn, dirty pantaloons and a checked shirt open at the chest, elbowed his way through the crowd. From the moment that Tom saw Legree approaching, he felt horror and revulsion. Legree had a round head; large gray eyes; and shaggy, sandy eyebrows. His large, coarse mouth was distended with tobacco. Periodically he spat tobacco juice. His hands were large, hairy, sunburned, freckled, and very dirty, with long nails. Legree seized Tom by the jaw, yanked his mouth open to inspect his teeth, made him pull up his sleeves to show his arm muscles, turned him around, and made him jump. "Where were you raised?" he asked Tom.

"In Kentucky," Tom answered, looking around for deliverance.

"What was your job?" Legree asked.

"I took care of my master's farm," Tom said.

"Likely story!" Legree scoffed and passed on. He stopped in front of Susan and Nancy. His heavy, dirty hand drew Nancy toward him, passed over her neck and breasts, and felt her arms. Legree looked at her teeth and then pushed her back against Susan, whose face showed horror. Nancy began to cry.

"Shut up, you!" Skeggs said. "No whimpering here."

The sale began. Louis was sold to Duchenne for a high price. Other St. Clare slaves went to various bidders.

"Up with you, boy!" the auctioneer said to Tom. Tom stepped onto the block. The auctioneer sang out his selling points. There was a rapid fire of bids in English and French. The gavel thumped as the auctioneer announced Tom's price, and Tom was pushed from the auction block. Legree seized Tom roughly by the shoulder, pushed him to one side, and said harshly, "Stand there." He then bought a woman named Lucy and five men.

Susan soon was sold. She went from the block, looking back at Nancy, who stretched her hands toward her mother. With agony Susan looked into the face of her new master, a respectable middle-aged man with a kindly face. "Oh, Master, please buy my daughter!" she pleaded.

"I'm afraid I can't afford to," the gentleman said, observing Nancy and looking genuinely pained. Nancy mounted the block and glanced around fearfully. The bids came rapidly. The gentleman joined the bidding, but the price soon was more than he could pay. He fell silent. Nancy was sold to Legree. Looking at each other for the last time, she and her mother wept.

Legree brought his eight new slaves, handcuffed, to a steamboat on the Red River. With chains on their wrists and ankles, they sat on the lower deck. In despair, Tom expected that he never would see his family again. Auguste and Eva were dead. Their home had been one of refinement, warmth, and relative ease. Now he belonged to an obviously brutal man.

"Stand up," Legree ordered Tom. Tom stood. He had been dressed for sale in his best suit, with well-starched neck linen and shining boots. "Take that linen off!" Legree demanded.

Encumbered by his shackles, Tom struggled to remove his linen. Legree roughly pulled it from Tom's neck. Then he unshackled Tom. "Take off your boots," he said. Tom did. Legree turned to Tom's trunk, which he had been ransacking, and removed an old pair of pantaloons and an old coat. Tom had worn the coat when he did stable work. "Put these on." Legree said. Tom went to a recess, changed his clothes, and returned. "Here," Legree said, throwing Tom a pair of coarse shoes. After Tom had put on the shoes, Legree refastened Tom's chains.

Legree started to go through the pockets of Tom's former clothes. He drew out a silk hand-kerchief and put it into his own pocket. Legree glanced at several trifles that Tom had treasured because they had amused Eva; he tossed these items into the river. Coming to Tom's hymn book, Legree contemptuously said, "Religious, huh?"

"Yes, Master," Tom said.

"I'll soon have that out of you. I won't have any praying, singing, bawling niggers on my place." Legree glared at Tom's downcast face and walked off. He took Tom's trunk to the boat's forecastle, where it was soon surrounded by deckhands. With much laughing at the expense of "niggers who try to be gentlemen," Tom's former clothes were quickly sold. Then the trunk itself was auctioned off.

Returning to Tom, Legree said, "I've relieved you of your extra baggage. Take good care of the clothes you're in. It'll be a long time before you get more. On my place niggers make do with one outfit a year."

Legree walked up to Nancy, who sat chained to Lucy. Chucking Nancy under the chin, he said, "Well, my dear, keep up your spirits." Nancy reacted with visible fear and revulsion. Legree frowned fiercely. "None of your airs, gal! You'll keep a pleasant face when I speak to you, do you hear?" Stepping back a few paces, Legree ordered, "All of you, look at me!" He held up his fist. "This fist has gotten as hard as iron knocking down niggers. I haven't ever met a nigger I couldn't bring down with one blow." Legree brought his fist so close to Tom's face that Tom blinked and drew back. "When I tell you to do something, you'd better do it quick. When one nigger dies, I buy another, so don't think I'll be coddling you." Lucy and Nancy drew in their breath, and the whole group sat with downcast faces. Legree turned on his heel and marched up to the steamboat's bar for a drink.

"Who did you belong to?" Nancy asked Lucy.

"Mr. Ellis. He lives on Levee Street," Lucy answered.

"Was he good to you?" Nancy asked.

"Mostly, until he took ill. He's been bedridden more than six months. He kept me up night after night tending to him. One night he became furious because I fell asleep. He said he'd sell me to the hardest master he could find."

"Did you have any family or friends?" Nancy asked.

"My husband's a blacksmith. Ellis hired him out. The trader took me away so suddenly, I didn't even have a chance to say goodbye. I have four children. Oh, God!" Lucy covered her face with her hands. Nancy wanted to say something comforting, but she couldn't think of anything.

CHAPTER 26

Legree and his new slaves disembarked at a small town. Legree, Lucy, and Nancy rode inside a crude wagon. Tom and the other newly purchased men trailed wearily behind, over a rough road. The road wound through dreary pine barrens, over log causeways, and through cypress swamps. In the swamps trees draped with black moss rose out of the slimy, spongy ground. Moccasin snakes slid among stumps and branches that lay rotting in the water.

Legree periodically drank liquor from a flask that he kept in his pocket. Laying his hand on Nancy's shoulder, he said, "Well, my little dear, we're almost home." The sexual look in Legree's eyes filled Nancy with dread and loathing. She pressed closer to Lucy. "You haven't ever worn earrings," Legree said, coarsely fingering Nancy's small ear.

"No, Master," Nancy said, trembling and looking down.

"If you're a good girl, I'll give you a pair. You'll have fine times with me and live like a lady, as long as you're a good girl."

The enclosures of Legree's cotton plantation rose to view. The estate had formerly belonged to a gentleman of responsibility and good taste. When the gentleman had died in debt, Legree had bought the place at a bargain price. What had once been a smooth front lawn with ornamental shrubs now was tangled grass. Here and there the lawn had hitching posts, where the turf was worn away and the ground was strewn with broken pails, corn cobs, and other litter. What had once been a large garden was overgrown with weeds.

The wagon rolled up a weedy gravel walk. Legree's large house was surrounded by a two-story veranda supported by brick pillars. Some windows had shattered panes or shutters hanging by a single hinge; others were boarded up. The ground around the house was littered with straw, decayed barrels and boxes, and pieces of wood. Roused by the sound of the wagon, four ferocious-looking dogs came tearing out. The two ragged men who ran out after them restrained them, with some difficulty, from attacking Tom and his companions.

"See what you'll get if you try to run off?" Legree said to the newcomers. "These dogs have been trained to track niggers. They'd just as soon chew up a nigger as eat their supper." Turning to a slave in a rimless hat, Legree asked, "How have things been going, Sambo?"

"Fine, Master."

Sambo and Quimbo were Legree's overseers. They hated each other, and the other slaves hated both of them. Legree liked to play Sambo and Quimbo off against each other, to ensure that they never teamed up against *him*. Both had coarse, cruel features.

"Quimbo, take these boys down to the quarters," Legree said, referring to the newly purchased men. Legree separated Lucy from Nancy. Pushing Lucy toward Sambo, he said, "Here's a gal for you. I told you I'd bring you one."

Horrified, Lucy cried, "Master, I have a husband in New Orleans!"

"So what? Won't you want one *here*? Go along now." When Lucy didn't move, Legree raised his whip. Lucy complied.

"Come," Legree said to Nancy. "You go into the house with me." Tom saw a woman glance from a window. As Legree opened the door, the woman said something in a sharp tone. Legree angrily answered, "You hold your tongue. I'll do as I please."

Tom and the other newly bought men followed Quimbo to the slave quarters, a row of dirty, dilapidated huts. "Here," Quimbo said to Tom outside one of them. Tom looked inside.

There was no furniture. The floor was bare ground strewn with dirty straw.

Late in the evening the huts' exhausted occupants returned from their labor in the cotton fields. Their clothes were soiled and tattered. In hoarse, guttural voices they contended for the few hand-mills available for grinding corn into meal. They had to make their supper—nothing but cornbread—from this cornmeal. They'd been in the fields since dawn, pressed to their utmost under Sambo's and Quimbo's driving lashes. Tom searched for a kindly face but found none. He saw only sullen, defeated, brutish expressions. The strongest among the slaves pushed away those who were weaker.

Tom was almost faint with hunger. "You!" Quimbo said to him, throwing down a coarse bag that contained a peck of corn. "Take that. You won't get any more this week." The sound of the corn-grinding continued late into the night. Tom waited until a late hour to get a hand-mill. Then, moved by the exhaustion of two women who were trying to grind their corn, he ground for them. An expression of surprise and gratitude came over their haggard faces. They mixed Tom's cornbread for him and tended its baking. "Find rest in the Lord," Tom said consolingly.

"I wish I knew where to find him!" one of the women said. "I never get any rest. I tremble all day. My flesh is sore. Sambo's always threatening me because I don't pick cotton faster. Every night it's almost midnight before I get my food. I feel I've just gone to bed when the horn blows calling us back to the fields. If I knew where this lord is, I'd tell him how much I need rest."

The women went off to their cabins, and Tom stumbled into the cabin that Quimbo had indicated to him. The floor already was strewn with sleepers. The air was foul. Tom wrapped himself in a tattered blanket, lay down on the straw, and fell asleep.

A few weeks after his arrival at Legree's plantation, Tom noticed a striking newcomer in neat, respectable clothes: a tall woman about forty years old. Her whole appearance was graceful and delicate, but her face was deeply wrinkled with lines of pain and proud, bitter endurance. Her complexion was sallow and unhealthy, her cheeks and body overly thin. Her large black eyes were filled with despair. As she walked toward the cotton fields with the other slaves, it was clear that they knew her. One of them exulted, "So you're joining us at last, Cassy. Serves you right!"

Laughing, another said, "You'll see how much fun it is, Missie."

"We'll see her work!"

"I'd be glad to see her flogged."

Cassy walked on, ignoring these taunts. All the way to the fields, she stayed near Tom, although she didn't look at him or speak to him. Tom soon was busy picking cotton, but he often glanced at Cassy. She picked cotton quickly and skillfully.

In the course of the day, Tom found himself working near Lucy. He heard her praying. She trembled and looked about to collapse. Tom came close and secretly transferred several handfuls of cotton from his sack to Lucy's. "Don't," Lucy begged. "You'll get into trouble."

Sambo came up. "What's going on here?" He kicked Lucy with his heavy leather shoe and struck Tom across the face with his whip. Tom silently resumed picking cotton. Lucy fainted. "I'll bring her to," Sambo said with a vicious grin, "with something better than smelling salts." Taking a pin from his coat sleeve, he buried it in Lucy's flesh. Lucy groaned and half rose. "Get up!" Sambo ordered. Lucy resumed picking. "See that you keep to it," Sambo warned, "or you'll wish you were dead."

"I already do," she thought.

After a while Tom put all the cotton in his sack into Lucy's. "Oh, you mustn't!" she cried. "God only knows what they'll do to you!"

"I can bear it," Tom said, and he returned to his place.

Cassy now took some cotton from her basket and hurriedly placed it in Tom's. Having seen Cassy's action, Quimbo came from across the field. "What do you think you're doing?" he said to Cassy. "You're under *me* now."

Cassy's eyes flashed. She drew herself up and looked at Quimbo with scorn. "Touch me if you dare! I still have the power to have you killed!"

Cowed, Quimbo said, "I didn't mean any harm, Miss Cassy."

"Keep your distance, then," she said. Quimbo quickly walked back to the other end of the field. Cassy turned back to picking. Before the day was through, her basket was filled and she had put large amounts of cotton into Tom's several times.

Long after dusk the weary slaves, their baskets on their heads, filed up to the building in which cotton was weighed and stored. Legree was there with Sambo and Quimbo. Sambo said to Legree, "That Tom is going to make trouble. He put cotton into Lucy's basket. He'll have all these niggers feeling abused if you don't watch him."

Tom was a first-rate field hand, but Legree disliked him. It was a case of evil hating good. Legree saw that Tom despised cruelty. He also saw that Tom's compassion was starting to affect the other slaves, who respected Tom. "He'll have to get a breaking in, won't he, boys?" Legree said. Sambo and Quimbo grinned. Rolling his tobacco around in his mouth, Legree said, "Make him flog Lucy."

"He won't do it," Sambo said.

"He'll have to. Did Cassy do her day's work?" Legree said.

"Yes," Sambo admitted.

Legree proceeded to the weighing room. Slowly the slaves wound their way into the room and presented their baskets to be weighed. Legree noted each amount on a slate that had a list of names pasted on the side.

Tom's basket was weighed and approved. Cassy came forward with her basket. As she delivered it, Legree looked into her eyes with a sneering but inquiring glance. She fixed her black eyes steadily on him and said something in French. Legree raised his hand as if to strike her. Cassy disdainfully turned and walked away. Tottering with weakness, Lucy delivered her basket. It was of full weight, as Legree saw. Pretending anger, he said, "You lazy beast! Short again? Stand aside. You'll catch it pretty soon!" Lucy gasped with surprise and fear and sat down on a board. "You, Tom, come here," Legree said. "I aim to make you an overseer. You might as well begin tonight." Indicating Lucy, he said, "Take this gal and flog her."

"I can't do that," Tom said quietly.

Taking up a leather whip, Legree struck Tom heavily across the cheek. Then he repeatedly punched Tom. "*Now* will you say you can't do it?"

Wiping the blood that trickled down his face, Tom said, "I'm willing to work hard every day, but I'll never flog someone. Never."

Most of the slaves were amazed. Lucy clasped her hands and fearfully said, "Oh, God." Slaves looked at one another and drew in their breath in anticipation of the storm to come.

At first Legree was dumbfounded. Then he exploded. "What, you black beast? You refuse to do as I say?"

"Flogging is cruel and wrong," Tom said.

"You think you're so pious!" Legree raged. "Didn't you ever read in your precious Bible, 'Servants, obey your masters'? Aren't I your master?" He kicked Tom with his heavy boot. "Sambo, Quimbo, give this dog a breaking in that he'll never forget!" Sambo and Quimbo laid hold of Tom. Lucy wept as they dragged Tom from the place.

Late that night Tom lay groaning and bleeding in an old cotton-gin shed, among pieces of broken machinery, piles of damaged cotton, and other accumulated rubbish. The humid air swarmed with mosquitoes, whose bites increased the pain of Tom's wounds. Tom also felt a burning thirst. Someone entered. Lantern light flashed on Tom's face. "Who's there?" he asked.

"It's me, Tom—Cassy," Cassy said.

"Please give me some water." Cassy set down the lantern. Pouring water from a bottle, she raised Tom's head and gave him water. He drained cup after cup. When he finished, he said, "Thank you."

Going to the door, Cassy dragged in a thin mattress over which she had spread linen cloths soaked in cold water. "Try to roll onto this," she said. Stiff with wounds, Tom took a long time to do this, but then he felt some relief from the cool, wet cloths. Cassy gently cleaned Tom's wounds and applied more cloths. Finally, she raised Tom's head onto a roll of damaged cotton that served as a pillow. "There," she said. "That's the best I can do for you."

"Thank you," Tom said.

Cassy sat on the floor, drew up her knees, and hugged them. She pushed her bonnet back. Long, wavy black hair fell around her melancholy face. "It's no use," she said. "You've been brave, and you had right on your side, but there's no use in your resisting. You're in the devil's hands."

"Oh, God," Tom groaned.

"There's no use calling out to God," Cassy said. "He never hears. Either there *is* no God, or he has no interest in preventing cruelty and injustice. I've been on this place five years. It's ten miles from any other plantation and surrounded by swamp. Legree could burn you alive, cut you into pieces, have the dogs rip you apart, or whip you to death. There's nothing that he's above doing. Nothing. I never wanted to live with him, but I've done that for five years. For five years I've submitted to his lust. Now he's lusting after a new gal. She's only fifteen and well brought up.

What's the use of your being good and brave and suffering as a result, Tom? You can't protect any of us, including yourself."

"I've lost everything—my wife, my children, my home, a kind master. He was going to set me free, but he died before he completed the process," Tom said.

"I've lost everything, too," Cassy said. "My daughter was sold years ago. I haven't seen her since. I don't even know where she is."

"Still, we mustn't become hard and cruel," Tom said. "I won't. I refuse to."

"Tomorrow they'll be at you again," Cassy said. "I know them. I've seen all their doings. Try to sleep now." After placing water within Tom's reach and making some additional arrangements for his comfort, Cassy left the shed.

Legree's living room was large and long. The once-fine wallpaper was torn, crumbling, discolored, spotted with beer and wine stains, and marked with financial calculations done in chalk. The room had a sickening smell of damp, dirt, and decay. Charcoal now burned in the wide fireplace. The dogs reclined amid the clothing and horse gear that were scattered around the room. Making himself a drink, Legree poured hot water from a cracked, broken-nosed pitcher into a glass of alcohol and sugar. He turned around to see Cassy. "So, you're back, are you? Either behave, or go out to the fields with the rest. Why can't you be friends with me?"

"Friends!" Cassy scoffed. When Legree had brought Nancy to the house, Cassy had pleaded for her. So far, Legree hadn't forced himself on Nancy. The night before, however, he had grabbed Nancy and started manhandling her. Cassy had entered the room and pushed Legree away. A fierce quarrel between Legree and Cassy had followed. Legree had said, "Stay out of this, or you'll be picking cotton." In a show of defiance, Cassy had gone to the fields the next day and picked cotton.

"Tom won't be fit for work for a week now," Cassy said. "You've lost one of your best field hands when you need him most."

"Yes," Legree admitted, "I probably lost money in having him beaten."

"Next time don't be such a fool," Cassy said, and she left. By way of a back door, she went up to Nancy's room. Nancy was sitting, pale with fear, in a corner.

When Cassy entered, Nancy exclaimed, "Oh, Cassy, I'm so glad to see you! I was afraid it was Legree. Isn't there some way to get away from here? I don't care where. Into the swamp with the snakes. Anywhere! I can't hold him off much longer. Soon he'll rape me."

"Everyone I ever knew who tried to escape from here has been tracked by the dogs and brought back," Cassy said. "You wouldn't sleep much if I told you what Legree does to runaways. I've heard screams that I haven't been able to get out of my head for weeks."

At dawn Legree went to the cotton-gin shed. Giving Tom a contemptuous kick, he said, "I told you I'd teach you a lesson. How did you like it?" Tom didn't answer. Kicking Tom again, Legree ordered, "Get up!" Tom struggled to get up. As soon as he was on his feet, Legree said, "Now get down on your knees and beg my forgiveness." Tom didn't move. "Down!" Legree struck Tom with his riding whip.

"I did what was right," Tom said quietly, "and I'll never do otherwise."

"How would you like to be tied to a tree and have a fire lit around you?"

"I'm not afraid to die," Tom said. "If you kill me, I'll just go to heaven that much sooner."

"I can give you a lot worse than dying!" With one blow of his fist, Legree struck Tom to the ground.

Having entered unnoticed, Cassy cried, "Will you continue to be a fool? Leave him alone! Let me get him fit to go back to the fields. Or do you want to lose *more* money?" Legree turned and left.

CHAPTER
28

Before Tom's wounds had healed, he was forced to return to the cotton fields. Day after day he suffered pain and exhaustion. All of the field slaves worked seven days a week. At the end of each day's work, Tom's head swam. If he tried to read his Bible, his eyes failed him. Tom prayed for deliverance. He felt compassion and sympathy for all the wretches around him. He continually provided assistance to others. On cold nights he would give his tattered blanket to someone shivering with sickness. At the risk of failing to meet his cotton quota, he often filled the baskets of weaker slaves with cotton that he had picked. Tom's kindness had a softening effect on the others. When the busiest season was past and the slaves had Sundays for their own use, they tried to hold prayer meetings. But Legree violently broke up these meetings.

One night after everyone else in Tom's hut was asleep, Cassy's face appeared at the hole that served for a window. She silently gestured for Tom to come outside. Tom went out to Cassy, whose eyes glinted with intense anticipation. "Come with me," she whispered, laying her hand on Tom's wrist and drawing him forward. "You can be free tonight!"

"What? How?" Tom said, disbelieving.

"Come with me. Legree's asleep. He had a lot to drink, so he won't wake up easily. The back door is unlocked. The door to his room is open. I'll show you the way. I have an ax. I'd kill him myself, but my arms are too weak. Come and do it!"

"Not for ten thousand worlds, Cassy," Tom said, stopping and holding her back.

"Think of all these poor creatures," Cassy said with a flash of anger. "We can set them all free. We can all go somewhere and start a settlement. I've heard of that being done. Any other life would be better than this."

"No," Tom said firmly. "I won't murder anyone, even Legree."

"Then, *I'll* do it," Cassy said.

"No, Cassy!" Tom pleaded. "Don't damn your soul. We should love even our enemies."

"Love!" Cassy exclaimed indignantly. "Why should anyone love the likes of Simon Legree? To love him would be to love evil."

"If you kill him, you'll be *doing* evil, Cassy. Put this terrible thought out of your mind. Are you sure there's no chance that you can escape?"

"Would you go with me?" Cassy asked.

"No," Tom said. "I would stay to comfort and help the others."

Cassy was silent. Suddenly she thought of a plan that never had occurred to her before. "I'm going to escape with Nancy, Tom!" she said. "We'll pretend to flee by way of the swamp, but then we'll double back through the creek and hide in Legree's attic. No one ever goes there. When they've stopped searching for us, we'll truly flee."

Legree's attic was a large, dusty space littered with cast-off lumber. A small window with dingy, dusty panes let in a small amount of light. Over several nights, when everyone else was asleep, Cassy brought food to the attic—enough to sustain Nancy and her for a week or so. Cassy also brought clothing and other items for their journey.

One evening Cassy and Nancy arranged two small bundles. "There. These will be large enough," Cassy said. "Now put on your bonnet. Let's go." Cassy and Nancy glided noiselessly out the back door and ran down by the slave quarters, knowing that the moonlight would suffice for Sambo, Quimbo, or Legree to see them. When they reached the edge of the swamp that encircled the plantation, Legree called to them to stop. Cassy and Nancy plunged into the swamp.

Hurrying to the quarters of the male slaves, Legree yelled, "Sambo! Quimbo! All hands! Nancy and Cassy have run off into the swamp.

I'll give meat to any nigger who catches them. Turn out the dogs!" Most of the men sprang into action. Men loosed the dogs, grabbed torches, and ran to the swamp. Tom was among the few men who stayed behind. The house slaves ran out to see what was happening.

"If we can't catch them, should we shoot them?" Sambo asked Legree.

Legree gave Sambo a rifle. "You can shoot Cassy, but not Nancy."

"Quick!" Cassy said to Nancy as she led the way to a creek that ran behind Legree's house. So that the dogs couldn't follow their scent, Cassy and Nancy waded in the creek until they were opposite the house's back door. They hurried in. Cassy took a key from Legree's coat pocket, unlocked his desk, and removed a roll of bills. "This will pay our way to Ohio," Cassy said. She and Nancy hurried up to the attic. When their eyes had adjusted to the near-darkness, they moved further into the attic. Cassy had placed two mattresses and two pillows on the floor. Exhausted from stress, Nancy soon fell asleep. After a while she was awakened by shouting, the tramp of horses' feet, and the barking of dogs. She started up with a gasp of fear. "It's only the hunt coming back," Cassy said. "We're alright. If you look out of this peephole, you'll see them. Legree has given up for now."

The stillness of midnight settled down over

the house. Cursing his ill luck and swearing vengeance, Legree went to bed.

The next morning the hunt for Cassy and Nancy resumed with horses, dogs, and guns. It was, of course, unsuccessful. Furious at having failed, Legree looked for a scapegoat. He chose Tom. He had noticed that Tom had refused to assist the pursuers. Legree ordered Sambo and Quimbo to bring Tom to the house. When Tom entered, Legree said, "I noticed you didn't join the search for Cassy and Nancy. Why not?"

"I wanted them to escape," Tom said.

"You wanted them to escape," Legree repeated through clenched teeth. "Did you help them escape?"

"No," Tom said.

"Did you know about it?" Legree asked.

Tom didn't say anything, but he cast his eyes downward.

"You knew! Do you know where they went?"

Again Tom said nothing but looked down at the floor.

"Where did they go?" Legree roared.

Tom said nothing.

"Tell me what you know!"

"I have nothing to tell," Tom said.

"Tell me, or I'll kill you!"

Tom stood silent.

Legree struck Tom to the ground. "Take him to the shed," he ordered Sambo and Quimbo.

In the shed Sambo and Quimbo tied Tom by his hands, with his arms spread. Then they beat and whipped him until he fainted. Sambo went to the house and told Legree, "I think he's almost dead."

Legree went to the shed and looked at Tom. "Take him down," he instructed Sambo and Quimbo. Tom was left lying, unconscious, on the floor.

CHAPTER 30

Two days later James Shelby drove a wagon up to Legree's house. He sprang out and asked for Legree.

By the time Ophelia's letter had reached Margaret Shelby, Tom had been bought by Legree. The letter had stated only that Tom was going to be sold; it hadn't named his new owner. Margaret had read the news with concern but had been preoccupied with tending to her sick husband, who had died of fever several days later. Margaret and James had taken charge of the estate. They had sorted out the accounts, sold property, and settled debts. Six months later, having business down river, James had decided to go to New Orleans to find Tom and buy him back. After some additional months, he had learned that Tom had been sold to Legree.

When James entered the house, he found Legree in the living room. Legree received him coldly. "I understand that you bought a Negro named Tom in New Orleans," James said. "He used to be on my father's farm. I've come to see about buying him back."

"Yes, I bought him," Legree said angrily. "Nothing but trouble! I had him flogged. I think he's dying."

James's eyes flashed. "Where is he?" he demanded. "Let me see him."

"He's in that shed," a small boy who stood holding James's horse said, pointing to the shed. Legree kicked the boy and swore at him. James turned and strode to the shed.

Tom had been lying in the shed for two days. Some slaves had secretly brought him water, but he lay near death. When James entered the shed, he felt dizzy with shock and grief. "Is it possible?" he cried. Kneeling down by Tom, he said, "Uncle Tom. My poor friend!" Tom slightly moved his head. James wept. "Uncle Tom, please live! It's James Shelby. Do you know me? I've come to take you home."

Opening his eyes, Tom feebly said, "Master James!" He looked bewildered. Then he realized that James really was there. "You didn't forget me!"

"Of course not. I've come to buy you and take you home."

"It's too late, Master James," Tom said. "God is going to take me now. I'm going to heaven, not Kentucky."

"No!" James said, sobbing. He grasped Tom's hand. "Please don't die, Uncle Tom. Please. We'll make everything come right."

"Don't tell Chloe how you found me," Tom said. "It would cause her too much pain. Just tell her that you found me dying from a fever and that I went peacefully. Tell her my work here was light and easy. How are my children?"

"They're fine, Tom, fine."

"How I've longed for them! Give them my love. I'm going now," Tom said softly, "going to God." He closed his eyes, breathed heavily, and died.

James wept for some time before walking angrily back to the house. "Tom is dead," he said to Legree, unable to conceal his anger and contempt. "Will you let me take his body and bury him?"

"His body's no use to *me*," Legree said indifferently.

While Cassy watched from the attic peephole, James spread his cloak in the wagon. Then he and some slaves carried Tom's body to the wagon and placed it on the cloak. "They've killed Tom!" Cassy exclaimed with grief. She and Nancy wept bitterly.

Turning to Legree, who was watching him, James said, "Tom's innocent blood will have justice, Mr. Legree. I'll report this as a murder. I'll go to the very first magistrate and report you."

"Do that!" Legree scoffed. "Who will be your witnesses?" Realizing that Legree would go unpunished, James fell silent. "Anyway, what's the fuss over a dead nigger?" Legree said.

James struck Legree flat onto his face and drove away. He buried Tom on a knoll shaded by several trees.

CHAPTER
31

That night Cassy and Nancy fled. Cassy was dressed wholly in black, in the manner of a Spanish Creole lady. She wore a small bonnet whose thickly embroidered veil concealed her face. Pretending to be Cassy's servant, Nancy walked behind Cassy, carrying a carpet bag and some bundles. Cassy and Nancy went to the inn where James was staying while he awaited the next steamboat. He was hurrying back to Kentucky.

Cassy's manner, refined way of speaking, and appearance of wealth prevented any suspicions that she and Nancy were runaways. When the steamboat came, James politely helped Cassy aboard and secured a good stateroom for her. Pretending to be ill, Cassy stayed in the stateroom, with Nancy, until the steamboat passed from the Red River onto the Mississippi. James, Cassy, and Nancy then transferred to the same northbound steamboat. Cassy now came to the dinner table and periodically sat outside her state-room. James was drawn to her. He found her face somehow familiar. He kept looking at her and thinking, "She reminds me of someone." James looked at Cassy so much that she started to think he suspected her true situation. Because of his behavior at Legree's place and elsewhere, Cassy liked and trusted him. She decided to confide in him. James heartily sympathized with anyone who would flee Legree's plantation. He assured Cassy that he would help her in any way that he could.

The stateroom next to Cassy's was occupied by a lady named Violet de Thoux. Having over-heard that James was from Kentucky, she sought his conversation. James, Violet, and Cassy sat outside Violet's stateroom conversing. Violet asked James about Kentucky, where she had once lived. Her questions showed a knowledge of peo-ple and things in James's neighborhood. "Do you know a man named Harris?" she asked.

"An old fellow of that name lives near us," James said. "We never had much to do with him, though."

"He's a large slave owner?" Violet asked with keen interest.

"Yes," James said.

"Did you ever hear of his owning a mulatto named George?" Violet asked.

"Why, yes! I know George well. He married

my mother's personal maid, Eliza. They have a beautiful little boy, Harry. I heard that the whole family escaped to Canada."

"They did?" Violet cried. "Thank God!" Bursting into tears, she said, "George is my brother."

"What?" James exclaimed.

"Yes," Violet said. "I was sold south when he was a boy. A good, generous man bought me and took me to the West Indies. He set me free and married me. Recently he died. I was going up to Kentucky to try to find and buy George."

"I've heard him speak of a sister who was sold south," James said.

"What's he like?" Violet eagerly asked.

"He's a fine man, of excellent character and keen intelligence," James said.

"And Eliza?" Cassy asked with surprising intensity.

"She's a treasure—beautiful, intelligent, and pious," James said. "My mother brought her up and educated her. Eliza can read and write. She also sings beautifully and sews and embroiders with great skill."

"Was Eliza born in your house?" Cassy asked.

"No. My father bought her during a trip to New Orleans and brought her back as a present for my mother. Eliza was about eight years old at the time."

Cassy touched James's arm and asked, "Do

you know the name of the people from whom your father bought Eliza?"

"I think the name on the bill of sale was Simmons."

"Oh, God!" Cassy cried, almost fainting with joy. "Eliza is my daughter!"

CHAPTER 32

Inquiring at Underground Railroad stations along the way, Cassy, Violet, and Nancy headed to Canada in search of Eliza, George, and Harry. At Amherstberg they found the missionary who had sheltered the family. Through him, Cassy and Violet traced the family to Montreal.

George, Eliza, and Harry had been free for three years. Eliza had given birth to a daughter, Debbie, and had grown somewhat more matronly in appearance. George was earning good wages in the shop of a machinist. Harry, who was very bright, was attending a good school. The family was living in a small, neat apartment on Montreal's outskirts.

A cheerful fire now blazed on their hearth. Covered with a white cloth, the dining room table stood ready for the evening meal. George sat at his desk in one corner of the living room. He was making notes from one of the books that ordinarily stood on the bookshelf over his desk.

He devoted much of his free time to study. "Come, George," Eliza said from the kitchen, where she was cutting a loaf of bread. "You've been gone all day. Put your book down. Let's talk while I'm preparing supper."

Debbie toddled up to George, pulled the book from his hands, and installed herself on his knee. "You little witch!" George laughed. Laying his hand on his son's head, George said, "Harry, how did you manage with those math exercises today?"

"I did them all, Father," Harry said proudly, "without any help."

"That's the way, Harry. Depend on yourself as much as you can," George said.

There was a knock. Eliza opened the door to see Cassy and Violet. Looking past Eliza, Violet saw George and rushed forward. "Oh, George!" she cried. "Don't you know me? I'm your sister, Violet!" Violet and George embraced, weeping.

Eliza and Cassy stood looking at each other. Then Cassy saw Debbie, who looked very much as Eliza had at the same age. Debbie peered up into Cassy's face. Sobbing, Cassy caught Debbie up in her arms and hugged her tightly. "My darling!" she cried. "I'm sure I'm your grandmother!"

Soon everyone was embracing and crying. During and after dinner, the adults talked and talked, pouring out their years of pain and longing, as well as the wonders of their escapes.

CHAPTER 33

James Shelby had hurried to the Louisville bakery where Chloe worked. When he arrived, he asked the owner for a private room in which to meet with Chloe. As soon as Chloe entered this room, James softly said, "Aunt Chloe!"

From James's tender tone, the pained expression of his face, and the sheer fact that he had come to the bakery, Chloe immediately knew that Tom was dead. "No!" she cried, collapsing onto the floor in a heap. "No!"

James rushed forward to embrace her. "Aunt Chloe, I'm so sorry. Uncle Tom . . ." James sobbed. "Tom . . . is dead, but . . . he . . . he died peacefully . . . of a fever. He wanted you to know how much he loved you and the children. He wanted you to know that his work had been light and that he was going to heaven."

Chloe wailed. "Oh, Tom! Tom!"

When Chloe had calmed down a bit, James—still embracing her—said softly, "You're free,

Aunt Chloe. I'll never own another slave. You're free, and the wages you've earned here are yours, for you and your children."

Chloe's tear-streaked face showed bewilderment. "I'm free? What do you mean, Master James?"

"I'm going to free all of our slaves," James said. "I want you to know that Tom didn't die in vain. His death made me realize…" James's voice caught. "His death made me realize what a terrible wrong slavery is. Come, Aunt Chloe," James said, rising and helping Chloe to her feet. "I'm going to take you home."

When James and Chloe arrived back at the Shelby estate, James hurried into the house for a private conversation with his mother. He had asked Chloe not to tell the slaves of their freedom. To his mother, James revealed the truth of Tom's death. The narration left Margaret horrified and weeping. Then James told his mother that they must free all of their slaves. "I've already told Aunt Chloe," James said firmly.

"You're right, James," Margaret said. "Slavery is a cruel, unjust, evil institution. When I think of what was done to Tom! I'll bear the guilt of that for the rest of my life. Call all the slaves together."

All of the Shelbys' slaves were called to the house's great hall. Having quickly learned of Tom's death, many were weeping. With great emotion James informed everyone that Tom was dead. Then he told them that they soon would be free. Tears of joy now mingled with those of grief over Tom's death. "The legal work will take a few weeks," James said, "but I solemnly swear to all of you that I will begin that work this very day."

A few weeks later, James again called all of the slaves together. He had a bundle of papers in his hand: certificates of freedom for every slave on the place. Amid the sobs and tears of all present, he read each certificate out loud and presented it to the person it freed. When every certificate had been presented, some of the newly freed people pressed around James and fearfully begged him not to send them away.

"My good friends," James said after calling for silence, "there's no need for any of you to leave here. We need as many farmhands and house servants as we did before. But you're now free men, women, and children. We'll pay you wages for your work. If my mother and I should fall into debt, you can't be taken and sold. You also can't be sold when we die. You're free now. If you stay here, my mother and I will do everything in our power to provide you with an education."

When James fell silent, some people cried out, "Thank you, Master!"

"I'm not your master anymore," James said. "I'm your grateful friend and, if you choose, your employer."

"Praise the Lord!" an old man cried, lifting his trembling hands. "Praise the Lord!" many others repeated.

"One more thing," James said. "I want you to know that Uncle Tom's death—his dying away from his family, friends, and home—made me resolve to free all of you. At Uncle Tom's grave I swore before God that I no longer would own slaves. So when you rejoice in your freedom, know that you owe it to Uncle Tom. Every time you think of your freedom, think of him. Let Uncle Tom's cabin be a memorial to him and a reminder to all of us to try to be as kind and good as he was."

About the Author

"**I**s this the little woman who made this great war?" Abraham Lincoln reportedly said in 1862 upon meeting one of his White House guests. The war was the Civil War. The woman was the internationally renowned author of Uncle Tom's Cabin: Harriet Beecher Stowe.

Harriet was born in 1811 in Litchfield, Connecticut. She was the seventh child of Roxana Foote Beecher and Lyman Beecher, a prominent Congregationalist minister. When Harriet was four, her mother died of tuberculosis.

Harriet was exceptionally well-educated for a woman of her time. From 1827 to 1832 she taught at the Hartford Female Seminary, a groundbreaking women's college founded and run by her older sister, Catharine. After her father became president of Lane Theological Seminary in Cincinnati in 1832 and the family moved to Ohio, Harriet taught for several years at another women's college founded by Catharine.

Just over the border from the slave state of Kentucky, the free state of Ohio was the first refuge for many runaway slaves. Ohio was a hotbed of controversy over slavery. In 1833 Harriet witnessed a Kentucky slave auction. She also visited a Kentucky plantation that would serve as the basis for the Shelby farm in Uncle Tom's Cabin. Tom and Chloe's cabin resembles the slave housing that Harriet saw: small log cabins, each with a garden. Just as Arthur Shelby makes Harry perform for Daniel Haley, Harriet's host made some of his slaves perform for his guests. Still, like Shelby, Harriet's host was a relatively kind "master."

In 1836 Harriet married Calvin Stowe, a theology professor at the seminary headed by her father. They would have seven children.

Active in the Underground Railroad, Harriet and Calvin sheltered runaways in their home. They also taught ex-slaves to read and write. Their maid Eliza was an ex-slave. She told Harriet of slaves being housed inhumanely, beaten, and raped. Like John Bird in Uncle Tom's Cabin, Calvin once drove across a dangerous ford late at night to bring a young woman fugitive to a house where she could safely hide.

At a Kentucky slave auction in 1844, Harriet saw a family torn apart: the father was sold to one plantation, the mother was sold to another, and their little girl was left, sobbing, without parents. Reflecting Harriet's intense feelings about the parent–child bond, many scenes in Uncle Tom's Cabin show a parent's grief at the loss of a child. In 1849 Harriet mourned her infant son Sam, who died of cholera. In Uncle Tom's Cabin, Mary Bird mourns her infant son; after opening a drawer filled with his clothes and toys, she weeps.

The Fugitive Slave Act of 1850 outraged Harriet. Expressing Harriet's views, Mary Bird declares, "It's a wicked law. I'll break it the first chance I get. What have things come to if a person can't give a warm supper and a bed to poor, starving creatures who have been oppressed all their lives?"

In 1850 Calvin accepted a professorship at Bowdoin College, so he and Harriet moved to Brunswick, Maine. Harriet started writing Uncle Tom's Cabin. Intended to persuade people that slavery was morally wrong, the work was based on written accounts of slavery, including slaves' narratives; Harriet's interviews of ex-slaves and others; and Harriet's own observations of slavery.

The first American novel with a black hero, Uncle Tom's Cabin initially appeared in weekly installments in a Washington, D.C. anti-slavery journal. In 1852 the story was published in book form. An immediate bestseller in both the United States and England, the book sold about half a million copies within the first year. One of the most effective pieces of protest literature ever written, Uncle Tom's Cabin increased opposition to slavery. Praised in the North and condemned in the South, the book heightened the tensions between North and South that would, within a decade, erupt into civil war.

In 1852 Calvin became a professor at Andover Theological Seminary. Harriet and Calvin then lived in Massachusetts until Calvin's retirement in 1863, when they moved to Hartford, Connecticut.

Although Harriet wrote short stories, poems, articles, and other novels, Uncle Tom's Cabin remained her most successful and important work. The book has been translated into many languages and never has gone out of print.

Calvin died in 1886. After about eight years of senility, Harriet died in 1896 at the age of eighty-five. By her own account, the greatest event of her life was the abolition of slavery.

About the Book

Uncle Tom's Cabin is about family: actual family but also family in the moral sense of those whom we treat as family. Harriet Beecher Stowe shows slavery's physical cruelty, from imposed exhaustion, cold, hunger, and thirst to beating, whipping, branding, and rape. However, she concentrates on slavery's psychological abuse, especially the separation of loved ones. The book's evil characters have little or no sense of family and cruelly sever others' emotional ties. The book's best characters cherish family and see family as extending beyond their own relatives and race.

Evil incarnate, Simon Legree apparently has no wife, children, siblings, or friends. He loves no one and disregards others' feelings. When he hands Lucy over to Sambo and she cries, "I have a husband in New Orleans!" Legree responds, "So what?" He has no respect for Lucy's marriage.

Similarly Walter Harris, another villain, has no respect for George's marriage. Harris keeps George from seeing Eliza and orders him to live with a different woman. On Harris's farm the little dog Carlo is George's "only comfort." Because George loves Carlo—sees him as family—Harris kills Carlo.

Slave traders callously separate mothers from their children. Stephen Marks recalls giving away a sickly child: "I thought the mother would be glad to be rid of him, but you should've seen the way she carried on." In the same vein Daniel Haley casually recounts, "I swapped a blind child for a keg of whiskey. When I went to take him from his mother, she jumped into the river with him. They went down and never came back up." Ted Loker says, "When I buy a child, I just put my fist to the mother's face and say 'One word out of you, and I'll smash your face in. This young one is mine, not yours.'" Loker feels nothing for such a child, who is his only in a legal sense. In contrast, most mothers love their children.

Marie St. Clare is an exception. Entirely self-ish, she loves neither her daughter nor her husband. In addition to being cold to her family, she has contempt for blacks, whom she abuses. She treats no one as family.

Although Arthur Shelby loves his wife and son, he doesn't see blacks as family or respect their family ties. "I'd hate to take the boy from his mother," he says of Harry and Eliza. But he does sell Harry. He also separates Tom from his family. Just as Legree dismisses Lucy's love for her husband, Shelby callously suggests that Chloe find another husband. It is only out of regard for his wife's feelings that Shelby doesn't sell Eliza. He has little regard for Eliza's feelings.

Margaret Shelby says that she'd as soon sell her own son as agree to Harry's being sold. Upon learning that her husband has sold Harry and Tom, she is indignant about the severing of family ties. She has taught her slaves "the duties of parent and child, husband and wife," she protests. "How can we turn around and sell [Eliza's] only child?" However, Margaret takes no action. She doesn't even warn Eliza or Tom. Similarly, when Chloe asks permission to go to Louisville to earn money with which to buy back Tom, Margaret laments, "You'd be leaving your children," but does nothing to provide the needed money. Even after her husband dies, Margaret doesn't try to get Tom back until her son has other business down south. In reality Margaret has little respect for the family ties between slaves. Unlike her husband, she considers slavery to be wrong, yet she goes along with the practice.

Auguste St. Clare, too, owns slaves although he believes slavery is wrong. When Eva asks him to free his slaves, he replies, "It's you I worry about." Insightfully Eva says, "That's the problem, Papa. You worry about only me while many people have nothing but pain and sorrow." Like all too many characters in the book, Auguste sees few people as family. He loves only one person deeply: his daughter.

Ophelia St. Clare loves Eva and Auguste and objects to slavery, but she initially feels contempt and loathing for blacks. When Eva kisses "Mammy," Ophelia expresses revulsion: "I believe in being kind to Negroes, but I can't imagine kissing one." She can't imagine any black as family. That changes, however, when she develops affection for Topsy.

At first Topsy loves only "candy and such." She says, "Otherwise I don't know anything about love. I never had any family." Topsy doesn't even know who her parents are. Through Eva's love and Ophelia's affection, Topsy learns to love—that is, to think of others as family.

John Bird is another character who grows. Having voted for the Fugitive Slave Act, he has a change of heart when Eliza and Harry arrive at his house seeking refuge. In defiance of the Act, John helps Eliza and Harry. He suggests that they be given some clothes previously worn by his wife and infant son, who has died. Morally John's family expands to include Eliza and Harry, and perhaps all other fugitives from slavery.

Even Eva grows in empathy. Early on she says to Tom, "It's a shame you had to leave your family. I'll ask Papa to let you go back some time." She does not say, "I'll ask Papa to free you so that you can return to your family." But later, when she is dying, Eva does ask her father to free his slaves, particularly Tom.

Chloe temporarily leaves her children in an effort to earn money for Tom's permanent return. She is a devoted wife and mother.

So is Eliza, who flees to prevent a slave trader from taking her child. "Harry is my only child," she tells Mary Bird. "I've never slept apart from him. He's my comfort and pride." Eliza's concern for others extends even to vicious slave hunters. When Loker is wounded, Eliza says, "Shouldn't we do something for him?" Although Stowe presents Eliza's concern for Loker as noble, many readers will find it misplaced because Loker is so cruel and unjust. Saving him makes it possible for him to continue to hurt and kill innocent people.

Another loving wife and mother, Mary Bird feels compassion for the oppressed. Outraged by the Fugitive Slave Act, she assists Eliza and Harry and would similarly assist any other runaways. Other exemplary whites in the book include Quakers who work in the Underground Railroad; Nicholas van Trompe, who has freed his slaves and who provides refuge for Eliza and Harry; and, at the book's end, James Shelby. James does the only decent thing that a slave owner could do: he stops being a slave owner. From childhood James has affectionately called Tom "Uncle" and Chloe "Aunt," but he truly sees the blacks on his farm as family only when he frees them.

George, too, is a hero. Although he grew up "with no family at all, no one who loved me," he's a devoted husband and father. "We'll be fine as long as we have each other and Harry," he tells Eliza. When his owner forbids him from visiting

Eliza and demands that he live with a different woman, George decides to flee and then work to buy Eliza's and Harry's freedom. He would fight to the death to protect his wife and son.

Like George, Tom dearly loves his family. "I thank God that I'm the one who's been sold— not you or the children," Tom says to Chloe. As he dies, he considers Chloe's suffering. "Don't tell Chloe how you found me," he requests of James. "It would cause her too much pain." Also like George, Tom sees other slaves as family. At Legree's plantation Tom is beaten for refusing to flog Lucy. He continually aids his fellow slaves. Tom is killed partly because he won't reveal Cassy and Nancy's hiding place. He sees all humans, including his white oppressors, as family. Tom loves the Shelbys, adores Eva, and feels "fatherly concern" for Auguste. Pious, he loves even Legree in the Christian sense of loving one's enemies. Like Eliza, Tom protects even people who consistently abuse others.

The expression "an Uncle Tom" refers to a black who is overly humble and subservient to whites. Why did the character Tom give rise to this expression? Tom doesn't recognize his own equality. He speaks and acts as if slaveholding "ladies" and "gentlemen" such as the Shelbys are his betters. Tom is a far better person than any slaveholder, but he has been taught to believe otherwise. He has absorbed some of his society's racism and class snobbery. Whereas George has a keen sense of justice and equality, Tom is somewhat in awe of aristocratic whites whose privileges have come partly at their slaves' expense. Stowe indicates that Tom would "lay down his life" for Arthur Shelby. Tom values Shelby more than he values himself. Further, in being willing to die for Shelby, Tom gives his oppressor more consideration than he gives his own innocent family, who love and need him. Tom lacks a fully developed sense of merit and justice.

Uncle Tom's Cabin encourages us to see all humans as family. For readers with a strong sense of fairness, treating others as family means treating them as justice requires.

**If you liked
Uncle Tom's Cabin
you may be interested in
other true stories in the
Townsend Library.**

continued on the following pages

Narrative of the Life of
FREDERICK DOUGLASS

An American Slave

Written by Himself

TP THE TOWNSEND LIBRARY

**For more information, visit us at
www.townsendpress.com**